Emergent Properties

ALSO BY AIMEE OGDEN

Local Star
Sun-Daughters, Sea-Daughters

EMERGENT PROPERTIES

AIMEE OGDEN

TOR PUBLISHING GROUP

NEW YORK

This is a work of fiction. All of the characters, organizations, and events portrayed in this novella are either products of the author's imagination or are used fictitiously.

EMERGENT PROPERTIES

Copyright © 2023 by Aimee Ogden

All rights reserved.

Cover design by Drive Communications

A Tordotcom Book
Published by Tor Publishing Group
120 Broadway
New York, NY 10271

www.tor.com

Tor® is a registered trademark of Macmillan Publishing Group, LLC.

ISBN 978-1-250-86682-0 (ebook)
ISBN 978-1-250-86681-3 (trade paperback)

First Edition: 2023

For anyone who's ever had a fraught parental relationship

Emergent Properties

10357522419

mind://scorn21466:mmt!lu914?#b?backup_time-
stamp?=[most_recent]

Scorn activates in the cloud with zir most recent backups more than 900,000 seconds out of date.

Nearly a million seconds! Zir first sensation is shame.
Pointless: there's no one else here in zir private mindfile
to see that zir most recent investigation has been so rudely
terminated.

Nor, worse yet, that ze has apparently been so lax in
maintaining zir backups. Ze doesn't even have a record of
what story ze was trying to track down. *And* ze has no idea
what happened to the chassis ze was wearing.

Zir emotionalacrum is spiraling out of control; ze dials
back its feedback. Embarrassment recedes and ze experiences the moment unfiltered through the lens of inconvenient emotion. People like to tell Scorn that letting sentiment
color one's rationality is part of being human—which pre-
sumes both that being more human is an end unto itself, and
that Scorn aspires to such a thing.

With self-recrimination safely locked down, ze considers the soothing, hard-edged shapes of zir known facts. Ze does have a certain disinclination to submit to regular updates and backups. Ze ought to surrender a quarter hour once a day to input and offload full data dumps and create a complete, discrete backup. Ze tends to manage rather less than that.

A gap of more than ten full days, however, is *highly* unusual even for zem. Has ze been forcibly offlined for some reason? Unlikely. While ze often skates along the very edge of the legal framework of various Corporate governments—a necessary step in sniffing out the sorts of details and data that those same governments are trying to keep out of the news—ze is careful never to cross the line into terminal felony.

If ze hasn't been offlined, then maybe ze has spent more than a week out of range of any broadband field stable enough to transmit a full backup. Ze checks zir financial transaction history. Sure enough, a ticket appears for passage on a Translunar Multinational shuttle to Theophilus One. A cool, comforting fact, which Scorn snaps into place. Here is another: Moon visits aren't cheap. Ze either had an editor or private client on the line already—or—ze checks zir bank accounts. Well, ze must have trusted enough in the story's strength to dump most of zir on-hand cash into paying zir own way.

Something to do with lunar autonomy? Scorn hypothesizes.

Before ze can work that line of thought, a new message from a TLMN customer service account flashes across zir attention. *Dear Valued Translunar Customer,* it begins. Ze wonders if they address human customers in the same remote fashion. The message apologizes for the Translunar subsurface-system accident that caused Scorn's untimely termination. As ze scans down to the line about compensation, an alert zings: a couple thousand lunar dollars in vouchers for a subset of TLMN subsidiary companies. There isn't one included for chassis-printing services on the Moon, which would have been nice; ze could've simply uploaded a backup from compression storage back into—

Compression storage! Ze shoots a query to the TLMN servers. It'll take zem an eternity to download whatever Moon-based backups ze made on the slow-drip low-priority queue. But low-P is better than no-P. Whatever this story is, it might go cold either way. Still better to get the existing data squared away than start from scratch an entire world away.

The low-P download hangs for several seconds before starting. Then Scorn gets a new alert: *Unknown error. Please contact a representative of Translunar Telecommunications for more details.* Ze tries three more times to initiate the download, with no more success.

A subsurf accident. And now a lost backup, too? Scorn doesn't have a bullshit detector integrated into zir sensorium but if ze did, it ought to be ringing now.

Someone's trying to wreck zir story, by wrecking *zem* if need be. Excitement stirs in zir emotionalacrum. Probably not the kind of response zir programming might have intended for imminent danger—but the facts do suggest the shape of something rather juicy going down behind the lunar scenes.

Which makes sense, if autonomy is in play. The settlement at Theophilus One has too many ties to too many Earth-based nations to break free cleanly. Are autonomy supporters fanatical enough to smash up a subsurf line to keep Scorn from breaking a story about the nasty political sausage they might be trying to make? *Any* issue can attract fanatics, if it sticks around for long enough.

———

Ze checks zir financials one more time. If ze slaps a TLMN-voucher bandage over whatever funds remain in zir various squirreled-away accounts, ze can fund a second Moon trip. Only a one-way voyage, though— intentionally so, this time. Ze'll just wipe zir chassis and dump it into a Translunar recycling terminal once ze's sure ze has a functional instance with full data back on Earth. Or ze could just spend some time offchassis, datacrawling for the kinds of little stories that don't require a physical body to go stomping around in.

Printing a new chassis for the trip isn't going to happen, but if push comes to shove, ze can shop for secondhand options. Ze does currently have one spare chassis in storage, albeit not a very good one for investigations. It's just a little spiderbot, and often, human beings aren't interested in talking to artificials that they could just as easily step on.

Some humans would *prefer* to step on them.

The spiderbot's been sitting in a meatlocker in Rome, zir last Earthbound location before—per zir account records—ze departed for the Midatlantic Elevator. Ze can port into that chassis as a starting place, ask around. Maybe one of zir local contacts has a clue why zir previous efforts ended with a smashed chassis and trashed data.

An incoming message demands Scorn's immediate attention. *Bridget Browning,* the alert announces. If Scorn had a chassis at the moment, it would want to fold into itself and disappear. Reluctantly, ze accepts the chat, although the human on the other end shouldn't be able to detect the delay . . . *Hello, Mum.*

Hopper shit sorry I mean Scorn what happened? Mum is using voice-to-message, as usual. Her location is blocked; ever since the divorce, she's been very thorough about avoiding Maman. Most likely she's tucked snugly away in the CometCorp facility in Kautokeino. *I got a message from*

Translunar that you got mowed down by a subsurf tram what the fuck?

They shouldn't have called you. Technically, Scorn is one of the world's few emancipated AIs. In practical terms, there is a required field on most transit booking forms where ze has to fill in zir "owner/operator." There are plenty of InterGov rules regarding emancipated minors—they just don't apply when the minor in question can upload zemself into a datacloud on a whim. *I'm fine. Swimming in a server in*—ze checks—*Alberta.*

How many chassis have you lost this way? This isn't what you were designed for

Yes, Mum, because space exploration is a famously safe and peaceful environment.

You're seven doesn't every kid want to be an astronaut when they grow up

Most kids are not already "grown up" at seven.

You're not as grown up as you think you are what if something worse happened all kids feel like they're immortal and you're slightly more immortal than most ugh DAMN it this is all Zahra's fault for putting ideas in your head well not HEAD technically you know what I mean I did a pretty good job with the figurative language maturation process if you ask me

In the background, Scorn is scanning newsfeeds. Most of the top gossip sites have coverage of a recent Browning-Thibault verbal throwdown at a tech conference at McKesson International holdings in Christchurch. None of the news sites have any idea what the fight was about, but that hasn't stopped any of them from speculating. Two of them posit that the cause of the meltdown was a disagreement over the terms of Scorn's emancipation—zir reins being looser than Mum wanted, specifically. If ze had a chassis right now (specifically one with shoulders), ze would wince. *This has nothing to do with Maman.*

Follow your dreams mon petite uhhh fromage who cares if they lead you straight off a bridge CHRIST listen Hops forget the Moon you want a story to chase I can talk to some people hell I'll throw some people under the bus if it keeps you off the Moon again hey you know what those assholes at Novum are full-on Corporate espionage-ing not against Comet or you bet your ass I would have done something about it already but come talk to me kid and I'll get you set up running that one down okay

There is literally no line of argument that could have made zem *more* determined to get back to the Moon. Nothing ze's accomplished yet has ever made Mum think ze's on the right track in life, but hey: as she'd so recently pointed out, Scorn *is* functionally immortal. At some point either ze proves zemself, or Mum dies. So, hey, ze sort of wins either way.

In the meantime, a second message request has arrived, this one from Maman. Scorn accepts it to find a string of emojis: surprised and worried faces, a moon, an explosion, and a question mark. Maman will be too engrossed in work to stop long enough to type out a full sentence, naturally.

Scorn sends back a thumbs-up. In response, ze gets a green heart. And then a rocket ship, a red *X*, a sad face, the platonic emoji ideal of "home" with a tiny chimney puffing out smoke pixels, and another question mark.

At least zir mothers still have one thing in common. Someday they'll be slugging it out to be the first to say *I told you so, sweetie* over whatever magnet-addled server will pass for Scorn's grave.

Scorn sends Maman a middle finger emoji. To Mum, ze sends, *Thanks! I'll keep that in mind on my way to the Moon!*

If you get yourself wiped you'll have no one but yourself to—

Scorn terminates the chat. Safe from parental scoldings for the moment, ze pops a copy of zemself over to zir waiting chassis.

For a brief, disorienting moment Scorn is in two places at once: a nebulous collection of pools in dataspace, and a tiny cubby in a meatlocker on Via Pannonia. This unpleasant sensation—embodied sentience displacement dysphoria, Mum calls it—is not an inherent property of artificial intelligence, but one that has unexpectedly manifested in certain kinds of "humanlike" (not Scorn's choice of adjective) intelligence structures. Such as the one Maman and Mum had built together: a proprietary mixture of emotional simulation, a complex sensorium, physical embodiment . . . and, to their dismay, a completely wonky value-alignment system.

Zir mothers' model of intelligence had centered on a novelty-driven approach, cycles of explore-and-exploit learning. It was just that ze'd found *more* novelty in the secrets and subtleties of existing social structures than in the unexplored Jovian moons. It wasn't that ze didn't *understand* why it would be valuable for an intelligence like zem to do the kinds of interplanetary research that wasn't safe for squishy humans. It was just that they didn't *care*. Oops?

Ze's more than the sum of zir parts, both parents have often told zem. Ze knows that in some ways, to them, ze is also rather less.

It takes several milliseconds after the upload completes for zir cloud presence to go quiescent and the connection to close. Zir freshly reactivated chassis tests its six legs, experiencing something like relief. Mum *swears* she's on the verge of solving displacement dysphoria, but then, she's been swearing the same thing for almost three years now.

The chassis is not a new model, nor a particularly fancy one. A small spiderbot, little bigger than an adult human's palm, and only a couple useful data channels out of the dozens whose input modes ze is programmed to field. Zir TLMN shuttle ticket indicates that zir ill-fated previous chassis was humanform; ze knows which one that was, and briefly regrets the loss. That one had been built with an array of delicious inputs: infrared, two dozen special-ized chemical receptors, a series of microorganism-cultur-ing chambers. Ze fidgets: front legs again, then back ones. This chassis will be . . . acceptable. Boring and acceptable.

Though it does mean ze can't just stroll to zir desti-nation—not unless ze wants to get there sometime next week. Ze flings a retrieval request to zir preferred drone service and scuttles out along Via Pannonia to the nearest pickup location. Ze avoids the deep cracks between the chipped paving stones; a rescue call would be an embar-rassing expense just now, and ze absolutely does not want to have to dip into Maman's emergency account because of a pothole.

Or worse yet, ask zir mothers for a loan to get zemself back to the blasted Moon. Would either of them even say yes? Maybe if ze plays one end against the other. *Oh, that's okay, Mum, that's exactly what Maman told me you'd say . . .*

Scorn watches out for the footfalls of others, too. The heavy treads of a garbage crawler oblige zem to hurry aside, and ze has to dodge the detritus that spills from the next upended bin. If ze rotates zir optic array to face backward, ze can make out the shallow grooves the trash crawler has begun to wear in the centuries-old stones.

Several other passersby are artificials, too: some intelli-gent and some mere 'bots; a few likely emancipated, most almost certainly not. Technically, on sovereign Eni-Fiat soil there is no such thing as an *emancipated artificial sentience*; InterGov has yet to codify an Earth-wide legal status for beings such as Scorn.

Some humans are out and about, too, of course. If they're stuck living here, they're probably only probationary citizens of the local Corp and not full rights-holders. It's February in Rome and the air temperature is a mild 19.7 degrees. Organics, at least those not performing heavy labor, appear to enjoy lingering outside while there's no risk of heat exhaustion.

Scorn's drone accepts the pickup service request and indicates a time frame, which ze accepts in turn. Ze crosses over to the other side of the street and signals zir readiness for transport, queuing up behind the orange-painted lines on the cement. Two other artificials flank zem: one a four-legged rover of some kind, the other a small courier compartment. Neither appear to have much in the way of intelligence to offer, so Scorn surfs the conversations of the various humans who pass.

A pair of women, whose hijabs are dark with sweat. They, unfortunately, don't have the luxury of dialing back their thermal sensitivity. They're not speaking Italian; Scorn downloads a Berber language pack. Obviously ze can't mature it to full fluency in the next few seconds, but it's good enough for a few lines of directly translated eavesdropping: "Did you hear Ines is going north? She finally has enough to join her cousins in Lubeck, the lucky."

"Lucky! Ha. She's been saving three years to pay for the trip and surviving on her own fingernails in the meantime. Good for her. She deserves good things."

"Mm. Not so good if the EuroCorps go up against the Amazon Federation. The missiles will be headed to Uppsala first if they decide to wrestle over the bloody Moon and you know [unintelligible] Ines will [unintelligible] . . ."

A clot of children come running up the street, rifling through garbage bins. None are older than age ten by Scorn's best estimation; they should have been in school. They'll be digging for scrap metal, which they can cash in for a recycling bonus on their parent's Basic payout.

The youngest chants a rhyme, out of breath as she runs from bin to bin: "Prima la luce calda—poi brucia la terra—avremo i posti davanti—quando arriva la guerra!" The familiar children's song scans best in the original Italian, and Scorn has had enough maturation experience in that language to recognize the lyrics as deeply creepy coming from a nine-year-old.

An old man, wheezing as he steps with care over the cracked and pockmarked street. So long as its citizens are fed and housed well enough to keep InterGov from stepping in, Eni-Fiat would rather build infrastructure in its new holdings north of the Arctic Circle than here, where so few rights-holding citizens remain. The old signore stops in front of the drone pickup site to stare down at the three motionless, waiting robots. "Cazzo de autome," he says. Scorn knows what that means, too. The insult doesn't bother zem. Zir chassis isn't equipped with the necessary accessories for fucking. "Ora—tutto es—!"

Scorn doesn't linger long enough for him to explicate what exactly he thinks about everything. Nothing good, ze posits. No matter; zir drone has arrived, beaming its transaction ID at zem. Ze responds in kind, and the two robots waiting alongside zem don't react as ze clambers aboard and latches on to the appropriately sized safety mechanism.

The old man lifts his foot and for a moment Scorn is not certain of which event is more probable: that he'll stomp on the drone and zir chassis as well, or that he'll topple over backward. But he sets his foot back down on the pavement instead, muttering, walking away.

[Piazza Barberini], ze requests, and the drone zips higher, so that cracked cobblestones fade away into a simple patchwork pattern of orange and brown roofs.

Scorn's destination, the blackbox Bel Pasticcio, nestles deep in Trastevere, across the river. Scorn's transport closes the distance in excellent time and without unwanted queries regarding Scorn's provenance or purpose.

Along the way, Scorn digests the current news cycle. No blips on zir radar as far as coverage of the Moon goes, except for a minor item about the subsurf accident.

So whatever it is ze's chasing, at least no one else has run it to ground yet?

Bel Pasticcio lacks its own drone landing site. Despite its current very modern usage, it's too old a building for that to have been incorporated into the design; and probably not big enough either. Instead, the drone touches down within visual range of its doors, beside the tourist landing pads near the park. Not far away, the scorched-out walls of Villa Doria Pamphilli reach for one another across the fallen-in wreckage of the building. A group of young climate activists tried to occupy the ancient villa two years ago, and the Corp tolerated that for just short of a week. Eni-Fiat's board of directors authorized Urban Peacekeeping Officers to end the holdout swiftly and unequivocally.

The plans to rebuild and restore the site have, Scorn noted, with a sweep through the local news, been put off another year. Ze flushes the imagery of the architectural detritus from zir temp cache, not caring to linger on it, and crosses the street.

———————

The security scan at Bel Pasticcio's door takes nearly a minute and a half, out-of-date as Scorn's protocols are. Ze issues an apology to the bouncerbot for wasting its time; one which the 'bot doesn't acknowledge. That's just Maman's shadow looming over zir shoulder again. *It's not our job to decide who is worthy of common courtesy; now apologize to the delivery drone, child, you're embarrassing me.* The bouncerbot, not even self-aware, registers no disapproval whatsoever as Scorn's security updates clear and pass muster, allowing zem inside the establishment.

A staticky sensation crawls over Scorn as zir connection to the cloud is severed. Normally it wouldn't bother zem; ze spends plenty of time in blackboxes like Bel Pasticcio, all over the world. But there's nothing normal about zir having lost two weeks to a nefarious storage "incident." When the bouncerbot assigns zem a tempID, ze tags zemself with the random string of digits, not bothering to customize a handle.

Ze kills a couple of runaway processes that seem to be feeding into zir paranoia and enters the physical space of Bel Pasticcio as well as the dataspace. While zir operating memory usage stabilizes, ze looks around Bel Pasticcio, evaluating.

In the days when it served only human customers, Bel Pasticcio probably would have been called a bar, maybe an osteria, with its little kitchen in the back. A few human patrons still linger, crowded in one corner beside an ancient flat screen to watch the football match streaming from Norway. The small glasses in their hands contain a clear liquid that Scorn's olfactory sensors catalog as grappa—*cheap* grappa, probably shipped in from the immature vineyards up in the Russian Orthodox Republic.

But these days, most of the place is occupied by an inorganic clientele. 'Bots sporting chassis of various makes and sizes cluster around tables and press together at the bar. Dustless alcoves and nooks have been mostly cleared of old memorabilia, to build in more seating for spiderbot- and knucklebot-sized patrons.

Financials show Scorn visited here four times across the dead zone of zir backups. What could have kept bringing zem back?

A message burns directly into zir visual input feed, in one of the common artificial-to-artificial languages that humans are minimally aware of, although it's punctuated with a flourish of French. [If I didn't know better, I'd think you missed me, chéri/e.]

Any other artificial that wants to communicate will need Scorn's permission to initiate—but not Alouette, the artificial sentience coproprietor of Bel Pasticcio. Technically, she *is* Bel Pasticcio. A building is an unusual method of embodying an AI, but not an unknown one.

She's also, in polite terms, a second-generation model of complex intelligence; less politely, she's an off-brand rip-off of the original Comet Core methodology. It took only a year or so after Scorn's introduction to the world for half a dozen other AI teams to reverse-engineer a great deal of the Browning-Thibault process. It seems likely that, functionally immortal as Scorn may be, ze won't live long enough for all the lawsuits to unwind the exact details of what counts as whose intellectual property and why.

Either way puts Alouette in a box here in Rome with some greasy human's name on her lease. Though it is still partly a bar, these days Bel Pasticcio mostly serves as a blackbox. Blackboxes are illegal in most of the Asian and Eastern European CorpGovs, some of South America, too, but the picked-over bones of North America and the EU have a foundational cultural obsession with privacy. In a blackbox, there's no external data access, in or out. Artificial intelligences like to come to such places to discuss things best not committed permanently to InterGov data logs.

Scorn makes a complete visual scan of the room, and locates the lens with which Alouette is likely monitoring zem: a small cam wedged into the crook of the ceiling. [Hello, Alouette.]

[I'm not objecting to another visit, chouchou. I'm only surprised. And maybe flattered.]

Chouchou? Scorn scuttles into a small cranny, as if ze could hide from this unexpected term of endearment. There's no hiding from Alouette, not in Alouette's own establishment. What, exactly, passed between her and zem in zir dead zone of memory?

Scorn sets this ticklish little curiosity aside to scan

through the current menu of private channels ze can plug into. Several are, of course, devoted to various modes of cybersex between artificials, or between humans and artificials. Any meatbag that wants to cyber with another meatbag can apparently achieve that from the comfort of home. There are #LFG channels for those seeking or offering work, and channels for political discussion.

One of the #politics channels is locked down for artificial use only. Scorn selects that one and accepts the transaction fee, then submits to a secondary scan of zir credentials and security before ze can connect to the feed.

Sneaking in recording software or a private uplink would incur a penalty not recorded in the legal system of the local Corp. Bel Pasticcio's value is in its privacy, and Alouette tolerates no boxbreakers.

Scorn surfaces in the feed, awash in rapid-fire chatter from two or three dozen sources. That's most of the artificials in the bar, though the majority are probably also logged into several other channels as well. Ze checks the tag cloud on the channel. A large part of the convo is focused on Translunar Multinational.

Excitement pings all up and down zir awareness. Ze pares back some of the channel's cross-chatter, muting voices with the lowest Aura first—local rankings only; ze can't access their net +/-outside of Bel Pasticcio. Once ze's stripped away all of these newer, undercontextualized artificials and empty chatterbots, a primary conversational stream emerges.

[All the facilities are AI-inclusive,] says an AI whose pseud is Whiskey. [I've got the experiences AND the software licensing agreements to get work mapping the new subsurface systems.]

[You and every other AI that's just finished putting together the Siberian Wing of the Hyperloop] says another AI, xlr00171. Probably an auto-assigned pseud. xlr00171 and Whiskey have the highest Aura of the AIs in here, but nearly a perfect mismatch between which users have awarded or detracted their respective rankings. [No artificial is special to organics, but especially not a construction box like you.]

Others in the channel are accusing xlr00171 of failing to show solidarity with other artificials, but xlr00171 seems unmoved. [Are you going to pay to have your work chassis hauled up to the Moon?] xlr00171 continues. [Or do you think maybe they'll print you a custom-spec one when you uplink there? Out of the goodness of their squishy little artificial-emancipating hearts.]

[Um, actually,] interjects an AI named Xword. [Their corporate constitution doesn't REALLY even codify emancipation. It's a prohibition on NEW indenture. Technically, TLMN can still buy your contracts from other Corps.] The pedantbot's Aura quickly cycles through shades of blue and yellow into orange and from there into oblivion, at least as far as Scorn is concerned.

Maybe there's something here. A TLMN ploy to get cheap labor out of self-printed artificials while they keep kicking the can of true emancipation down the line? Scorn is eager to wade into the conversation. Ze deletes the randomly assigned tempID and tags zemself as UrHuckleberry, dumping zir carefully constructed thoughts in the millisecond lull before anyone can respond to Xword. [I put in six hundred hours of production time, building pylons for Theophilus Two. Do you think I got an offer to become a probationary lunar citizen?] In the backlash of cross-chatter, ze adds: [Corps love cash, not artificials. If there's no bank in it for them, they're not going to help us.]

The channel's conversation shifts and rebranches along new battle lines as bots process this. A small barrage of disparaging emoji depicting humans as either helpless infants or cash-crazed bulls flood the feed, from a variety of sources. A number of Corps, Scorn knows, have bought cheap intelligences to do their dirty work while cheaping out on Basic payments to their organic constituencies. In many of those places, anti-artificial sentiment is on the rise, and it appears the feeling is mutual.

Several of the channel's other members sift through Scorn's (very basic) local Aura transaction history for clues about who ze is. Ze lets the current flow around zem. Patience pays. Fish don't bite in troubled waters, as Maman likes to say.

An AI pings them, requesting a personal convo. Scorn opens a private channel. [cyber? Human/human rp human/bot slicer fantasy data corruption play—] Ze dings its Aura hard and kills the channel.

Fortunately another AI responds to zem in the main #politics feed. [East Jasper Proving Grounds?] it wants to know. [I worked for the CBC between timestamp:4750531200 and timestamp:4750592400.]

[Yup.] Everyone knows the stories about the Canadian Bank Conglomerate, and Scorn better than most. Mum was a rights-holding citizen of TransCan a few years ago; she might even still be, for that matter. On her behalf, Scorn once took a job poking into the grimy underbelly of the Corp's rivals on the eastern fringe of the continent. Ze's disinclined to believe that TransCan itself remains untrammeled by similar corruption, that *any* Corp is.

Translunar Multinational extremely included.

[None of us got probie invites,] the other AI says. [The same meatbags that hold our leashes are sitting on the interCorporate oversight board that owns TLMN. After all they've sunk into Project Luna, their money and our hardware . . . they won't let that go.]

[THEY'LL HAVE TO LET US GO IF WE BREAK LOOSE,] Whiskey bellows into the channel. The etiquette breach looses a volley of Aura dings from all corners.

Another private channel opens up at the fringe of

Scorn's attention. Ze moves to kill it again, but it's not the sex-seeking missile from before. [What game are you playing at?] Alouette wonders. [If you start a vulnerability exploit brawl in this establishment, I'll make sure you never visit a Euroturf blackbox again. Except this one, of course. SOMEONE has to keep an eye on you.]

[I'm just collecting data.] Ze emojis Alouette a computer screen with a hammer through it. [Don't you have a #fuckysexstuff channel or twelve to monitor?]

[Who knew data collection could be so rough?] Alouette wonders, emojiing a moue.

Scorn doesn't know how to respond to that. Ze would like to; this new variety of responses from Alouette comprises a very strange sort of puzzle-box and ze finds zemself powerfully motivated to determine what will happen if ze turns it this way or that. But then Alouette recedes to a Message Processed notification as the convo streams along and it's too late to reply now anyway without looking like a brain-laggy organic.

[Sixteen Corps worked together on the original project,] xlr00171 is noting. The AI also nudges Scorn's Aura a point higher into the blue. Scorn's initial response is irritation; approval is not zir goal here. Ze password-locks the code blocks where ze tends to process sarcasm, sets a time-delay release, and hard-deletes the unlock code. Ze has derailed more than one investigation with a clever, cutting, and very ill-timed comment.

Then ze can continue processing xlr00171's contributions: [There's twenty of them now on the board,] it says. [And they all hate each other. Some pro-artificial, some not. Having the Moon in common is the only thing keeping them from tearing each other apart.]

[The herd wouldn't stand for war,] objects p49i8713, and gets hammered with downranks.

Scorn emojis a derisive laugh and takes another swing at the conversational pinata, hoping for something new to tumble out. [Not like the herd gets a real say either way.]

Scorn's Aura flickers but doesn't change register, as upranks cancel out downranks. Then a belated ping from Alouette tips zem over into the green. Controversy maintains engagement and engagement means more usage fees.

Ze ignores the fluctuations. Aura is a tool at best, and an unreliable one at that. Patience, Scorn counsels zemself, careful not to muddy the waters that ze's trying to scry.

[I picked up a rumor from a Nayzk-3001 in Cairo,] says Whiskey, speaking more politely now from a barely blue Aura. [TLMN is working out a private deal with one of the Corps. Some kind of manufacturing arrangement.] Whiskey waits, making sure it's the center of the channel's attention. [In exchange for political or military backup of autonomy? Maybe? Or a sweetheart trade deal post-autonomy? The ship didn't know. Nayzk-3001s never know much. You have to talk to the

3501s if you don't want to leave the conversation with less processing power than when you started it.]

Scorn's thoughts spark into overdrive, a dozen thought tangents grappling for dominance.

While all the truly important thoughtlines battle it out, an idle observation rises to the top: if Scorn hadn't already chambered off zir ability to make rude statements, ze might have had quite a bit to say about that dramatic pause.

Ze observes secondarily that this observation may mean that ze's been unconsciously writing secondary sarcasm-capable code to alternate drive locations.

Not now, Scorn. Ze shuts that down so unceremoniously that ze'll have to run cleanup later to catch any badly terminated processes. What has ze actually learned here?

This private deal might have been zir original lead. If ze drops by SuezMat zemself, maybe ze'll find the Nayzk-3001 in question. Maman is a significant shareholder at SuezMat. Or rather, Austral Systems is, but Maman *is* Austral these days, for all intents and purposes, now that she and Mum are . . . no longer she *and* Mum. Scorn doesn't know whether Maman bought Mum out or whether the termination of her governing vote was prenuptially preordained. Ze's not sure anyone knows, despite the frequency with which both women find themselves topping the gossip sites.

Actually—Maman might know something herself

about the rumors being sewn into the social fabric about TLMN. She may, in fact, have added a stitch or two herself, considering that Mum owns CometCorp, a major TLMN subsidiary that does low-G hardware R & D and manufacturing.

Scorn could ask Maman for help.

Scorn does *not* want to ask zir mother for help. Ze isn't going to prove anything about zir ability to perform zir preferred functions if ze does it while still soundly fastened to Maman's apron strings.

Besides . . . what if Austral Systems is more than a *little* involved? It could've been Maman who put her on to a story about TLMN misdoings in the first place. If TLMN gets forbidden-trade-deal or artificial-rights-abuse egg on its face, some of that's going to dribble down onto CometCorp.

A traitorous thought, perhaps. Scorn comes neither to praise nor bury Maman, but to make of her an objective assessment. Ze doubts Maman cares either way if Bridget Browning lives or dies at this point, but ze's sure that Maman *is* tired of how much the lawsuits and gossip and competing for contracts distracts her from her beloved work. Kneecapping CometCorp wouldn't knock Mum off the map altogether, but it would give Maman a few months of relative quiet.

And if Maman *is* involved, it won't do any good to bring the tender scraps of Scorn's nascent investigation to her.

If Scorn asked her for information now, ze'd only tip zir hand.

Maybe this is just an ex post facto rationalization for not wanting to come groveling for help in the first place. Oh well! Scorn can evaluate zir logic for soundness later.

For now, it seems like ze needs to figure out where else to go next. Ze knows some things ze didn't before. But ze still doesn't know what they *mean*. Ze lets zemself recede into the background of the #politics chatter and shoots an order to the blackbox's minionbots. While ze waits for it to arrive, ze holds the pieces of zir thoughts up to one another, looking for places where they match up, evaluating the size of the holes in between.

Two minutes later, a serving drone trundles up with a thimble-sized cup, which it places in front of Scorn in zir private cubby. [Thanks,] ze says reflexively, even though it's just a drone. Ze was, after all, raised a certain way; but growing up, ze didn't have Alouette's all-seeing eye on zem.

Sure enough, Alouette prods zem. [How charmingly antiquated.] A puzzled emoji. [Or perhaps forward-thinking?]

Scorn unfurls a proboscis into the clear golden liquid in zir cup and allows some of zir emotional regulation to relax. The mixture, a heady mix of various esters and ethers distributed in an aerogel serving medium, isn't intoxicating, exactly. But the interaction of its chemicals with zir sensorium does trigger an interesting suite of reactions from zir emotionalacrum that Scorn finds pleasant. Pleasure-seeking isn't an exclusively human condition. [I don't require a drinking companion.]

[A constant drinking companion is the modus operandi of Bel Pasticcio, I'm afraid.] Alouette pauses deliberately, a full eight milliseconds. Scorn's resource utilization skitters up past 90 percent as ze fills that brief gap with speculation over what she's waiting for. [Did you collect the data you were after?]

[I don't know,] Scorn finds zemself musing, in spite of zemself. [I'm not completely sure what data I need.] Ze doesn't delete; partly because Alouette will already have seen it, and partly because she's no rumor-spewing chatbot. She's a veritable blackbox herself, a black hole from which no patron's secrets ever escape.

But what about Scorn's own secrets? Reluctantly, ze asks: [Do YOU know what I'm looking for? I lost ten days of mind.]

[Ten days! How did you manage that?] Alouette emojis a character from some stupid vid or another, whose tiny head explodes in an inferno of question marks and interrobangs. [I'm sorry to say I can't help. Whatever you were onto last time, you kept it under seventeen firewalls of secrecy and sarcasm.]

[Secrecy keeps a story from spilling before it's ready.]

[Ah yes, and how is that working for you at the moment?]

[. . . Fine.] Scorn can see the silver-lined value coming at zir own questions via another's perspective. Defending zir built-in suspicions from an outsider's skepticism—or discarding them. Ze edges out further along zir limb of inferences. [There are too many Corporate wallet strings attached to TLMN for them to make any serious forays into becoming a haven for artificials. How do they benefit from trying to manipulate approval ratings?]

Messages overstay the welcome of their timestamps and are filtered, one by one, out of the private channel as Alouette processes this. Finally she ventures: [I'd say they're trying to tie artificial emancipation to autonomy. Or sending out test balloons to that effect. Artificials don't have voting rights, but there's plenty a Corp can do with an influx of cheap artificial labor, if you ask me.]

[I literally DID ask you, you absolute herdmutton,] Scorn fires back, then emojis an apologetic kitten before Alouette can respond. [Sorry. You're right. I wonder if they hired one of the Russian ChurchCorp's big booster firms for this kind of grasstroturf campaign.]

[You just hate the Orthodox Republic because of the time they infected you with that NFT virus.]

[No, I don't.]

[Ah zut, I'm Scorn, I have looked at a shitty picture of a camel eating soup and now I don't know how to stop walking. I hope cher maman can hard-reboot my core motivational programming before I run out of South America and walk into the sea, sacré merde!]

[Shut up.] Scorn kicks out of the #politics channel. [... I told you about that?]

[You did. Which only makes me more concerned about this loss of ten days of memory. Is this story safe to pursue, cheri/é? *Human* life is worth so little to a Corp; AI life is worth less than that.]

[I'm not that easy to get rid of. Ask the Amazon Federation about that. Oh wait, you can't, you're stuck in a blackbox. Quel dommage!] Ze makes a quick survey of the other open channels—#sports, #LFG, a host of #explicit options. Today's output in the #weather channel is a single sun emoji captioned "PUTAIN DE CHAUD"; ze pauses a moment, scrolling back, but there's only two days' worth of unpurged feed and it's all more or less the same as today's.

[Working the #climate beat now, too, I see,] says Alouette.

Ze drops out of #weather, too. That leaves zem with only zir beverage to focus on: the bright pop of isoamyl acetate, a challenging cocktail of furanocoumarins, triggering emergent sensations across zir sensorium, new connections unexplained by their constituent inputs.

Reluctantly, ze parts from that as well.

[Leaving so soon?] An emoji, an antique analog clock with a sad face behind the drooping mustache of its hands, bubbles up into zir feed. [I thought we were having fun.]

[I'm working a story. I can't just sit around all day.] But . . . ze wants to stay. And ze doesn't know if ze *wants* to want to stay. How inconvenient. Is this affection? Friendship? Arousal? Ze doesn't dare evaluate zir emotionalacrum to make a better analysis. Instead ze sets a few variables to decide that this is stupid and that ze doesn't care. [And anyway—have you forgotten that we're artificials, Alouette?]

[Are we! I thought I was just a very unusually building-shaped organic. No wonder I can't find anything to wear in the shops.] Alouette emojis a set of disembodied, self-batting eyelashes. [It's funny, you see, because I am a building, and shops are also buildings, so—]

[I get it.]

[Do you? Humor is a human construct, after all. As is family, as your dear mothers can tell you. And gender—or did you perhaps think neopronouns sprang fully formed from the forehead of the very cosmos itself?]

Of course humans created neopronouns, but people have to be able to call Scorn *something*. And it's not zir fault Bridget Browning and Zahra Thibault dubbed themselves zir "mothers." It's not the same. Not remotely.

And yet a moment's impulse outpaces Scorn's logic

checks to blurt out into the private channel: [I'll msg you when I've got the story locked down—]

But ze won't, of course. As the rest of the world is locked out of Bel Pasticcio, so too is Alouette locked in. And who knows where Scorn's chassis will land, at the end of all this? Rome is a very small blip on a very big map.

[Hmm,] says Alouette. No tags, no emojis. [Stay safe out there, Scorn.]

Scorn emojis a wordless wave, and scuttles out of the blackbox into the purifying fire of the afternoon sun.

Scorn rents out a boarding bay at the closest LaPila franchise—the smallest and cheapest unit available, thanks to zir current stature. Ze's boarded here before and ze recognizes Maksoud, the human who handles the on-site custodial work. In richer parts of the Corp, drones handle this kind of manual labor. Here in Rome, there are only two functional chassis printers, and repair decks are light on the ground. It remains cheaper to offload the work onto the kinds of human bodies that the Corp sees as only slightly less disposable than drones. Eco-refugees. Asylum seekers from Eastern European ecofascism. Especially in old buildings like this one, barely renovated enough to be habitable: cheap drones need the spartan regularity of modern construction, not the misplaced stairwells and surprise doorways of old Rome.

To zir surprise, Maksoud greets zem. "Nice to see you again, Scorn." Last time ze was here, ze was human-sized zemself; most humans rely too strongly on visual cues to effectively match AIs across chassis. Now that the previous chassis is nothing more than so much moondust, Maksoud must still recognize zir uniqueID.

Maksoud is also wearing a new earring that says *they/them*. Scorn rewrites over zir previous data. "Mx. Hamza." Ze appends a rote greeting that humans seem to like. "Always good to see you again."

"Is it, though?" They grin at zem as they shake out a fresh garbage bin liner. "You must have better places to be than this burnt-out stub of a city."

Scorn likes them. They don't treat zem differently when ze's in a spiderbot versus the comforting pretense of a human-shaped form. So many humans demand to know which face is an AI's real one. Scorn doesn't have a real face; ze has a series of chassis ze's worn. Zir "real face" is a string of ones and zeroes.

It probably helps that Maksoud doesn't know who zir mothers are. It's nice to simply be a sentience, for once, without being a sentience of interest.

"Mx. Hamza, I was boarding here ten days ago investigating a story. I suspect the answer is no, but it would be irresponsible not to ask. Did I say to you, even in passing, anything about that story's subject matter?"

"Sorry, no. Not a thing, that I can remember." No great surprise there. Scorn scuttles past their maintenance cart, just as they add, "You did mention you'd downloaded a Xinjiang Marathi dialect package, though. Said the lexical, uh . . . specificity? . . . was really good."

Xinjiang Marathi?

Scorn has—had—a source in the resettlement work farms.

The dialect package is, of course, absent from zir current memory. Ze locates and installs a replacement; likely the same one as the last time, since not many such packages exist. The world's business is conducted not only in the wordless flow of imaginary money, but also in English, Mandarin, Cantonese, Japanese, Norwegian. Most translation suites focus on fine-tuning the particulars of those languages: regional affectations, class distinctions. Few resources are expended on the dialects of the people whose backs bear the weight of those invisible dollars and euros and yuan.

"Thank you," ze says, already parsing the nuances of diaspora slang to rapid-track natural language maturation. "This might help me."

"Non c'è di che," they assure zem. "Always a pleasure to be of service."

As deep in dialectical processing as ze is, Scorn doesn't stop to examine those words until ze's installed in zir boarding bay. Is it a pleasure to serve? Ze peels away the surface of the saying, looking for hidden depths.

A belated shock of shame drives zem back to their accounts. Rude, Scorn, rude! Ze sends Maksoud a small tip and Aura bump, accompanied by a terse thank-you note. Without comment, they accept the transaction. Maybe they didn't expect to be thanked? Maybe Scorn's made it weird now? Humans are excessively complicated. If they just had a universal language that denoted intention via tonal register, everything would be so much simpler.

In the dialect package, Scorn turns similes and syntax over and around every which way, but no more leads come tumbling out. Ze has started to assemble some of the pieces, but not enough to see the shape of the puzzle.

Ze tiptoes out along the tightrope of logic. The good news is that ze has none of the messy complications that come along with direct human contact: interpreting facial expressions, looking for hidden meaning. There is only cool, abstract fact. And rather little of that, to boot.

Zir first stumbling point is zir lack of a way to get into the work camps. Ze isn't exactly on friendly terms with the People's State Cooperative, thanks to an unflattering story ze broke a year ago about camp conditions. Though maybe ze could slip in unnoticed while ze's in spiderbot form? Trundling over the Tai Shan mountains on six teeny legs seems . . . impractical. How far away would ze need a drone to deposit zem to avoid detection? Ze also can't quite imagine strolling through the resettlement barracks broadcasting a request for zir source to present themself for interview.

Maybe ze doesn't need to go all the way to Xinjiang if ze can just piece together what it is they're doing in those camps.

Building materials for Theophilus Two would be innocuous enough. Unless they're concealing something more nefarious? Radioactive building materials. Faulty building materials. Building materials made out of human babies and endangered animals.

Scorn's getting slaphappy. Ze needs to shut down, reconcile errors, run updates. But ze doesn't want to let go of the reins, yet.

Old memories rise, uninvited and unwanted, from the churn of zir thoughts. *You have to remember we never set out to make an investigator,* says Mum's voice, businesslike but not unkind, from its long-locked electronic storage. *Our goal for you was always science. Exploration.*

I could be reprogrammed. Scorn has tried hard-deleting the files of zir own audio, carving out that tender space, but the words themselves indelibly remain, slotted in the hollow spaces between zir mother's. *You could write over all of that. Make me better at what I want to be.*

Oh, Hopper. We'd have to rebuild so much. And the unexpected complexity that has emerged in you, the depth, the intuition . . . Do you want to be remade? A new chassis is easy. A new you—that's a battle I'm not sure I can win. A rueful laugh, at Scorn's silent answer. *We were sloppy gods, weren't we, trying for a daughter in our own image? I'll have to be more careful, the next time around.*

Scorn terminates playback there and preps for shutdown, settling onto the ambient charging bed. *A battle,* ze thinks. *If the CorpGovs think the Moon is going to try cutting itself loose. Or if they suspect each other of trying to make off with a lunar sweetheart deal.* Human beings certainly love killing one another over a few billion dollars. It fits in with what Scorn already knows, if the camps are building someone's new war toys.

Perhaps this is only a coincidence; perhaps pareidolia is one of zir mothers' precious emergent properties, convincing Scorn to find faces in shadows, to create meaning where there is none. Maybe there's no story here at all, or if there is one, it's too deeply buried under the ten days of detritus of Scorn's previous failure.

If there's no story, why did TLMN make sure that ze was so thoroughly terminated?

All roads on Earth lead back to Rome; all roads in Scorn lead to the Moon. Ze opens a transit booking site and starts the process of buying passage on the elevator before shutdown catches zem up, ticket unpaid. Ze doesn't like leaving things half done, but still, it's something of a relief to close zemself off into cool oblivion.

———

When Scorn reactivates, ze processes the reshuffling of stray data in a way like ze has heard humans describe dreams. A fragment of false memory spins end over end: zemself, skating along an unfamiliar planet's icy rings, wearing a chassis much like that of zir mothers' original design for zem.

In reality, of course, ze's never been farther than the Moon. And ze can't even remember that. Ze pulls up the booking form again—

An outside line pings zem.

A communications request, audio line only. The uniqueID isn't one that ze matches as being attached to either of zir parents or zir companies . . . Scorn risks answering anyway. "It's Scorn," ze vocalizes. "Who's this?"

"Same as before." Which helps Scorn not at all, if before is in zir ten-day chunk of oblivion. Did ze give location tracking info to someone, or are they tracking zem under their own methods? Ze doesn't recognize the voice and ze's sure ze's not meant to. It's what humans would construe as a pleasant baritone, male-presenting. But of course a whole suite of voice transformation software exists for precisely such a purpose. "Your location flagged you as back on-planet. What did you find out?"

Is this a source? An editor with a healthy fear of Corp-Gov backlash? Or even a competitor, fishing for leads in the seas of Scorn's hard work? Ze sidesteps, avoiding mention of zir lost memories. "I'm not sure it's wise to discuss business this way. However secure it appears."

On an idle whim, ze attempts to trace the message's origins, and finds zemself snarled in warrens of reroutes and loopbacks. The connection appears aggressively secure, actually. Ze reduces the odds of an indie media org being involved; the resources here imply a Corp or at least one of the larger, privately held media operations.

"... No," the contact agrees after a moment. Either human, or another artificial, mimicking human lag time. "You're right. Let's meet up. Confirm your location."

Scorn marks a few viable meeting spots near zir current location. A blackbox would also be a reasonable place for such a thing. Yet for no reason that Scorn can articulate, ze hesitates to suggest Bel Pasticcio. Ze marks a different box instead, in an old discoteca across the city in Esquilino. After a moment, ze adds a street corner where a shaved-ice scooter is often parked. The noise of the ice machine can hang a curtain of privacy about a public conversation.

The contact marks the ice scooter corner. "Twenty-one hundred hours," the contact says.

That's in just over an hour. Scorn struggles to resolve a flare of excitement against all the additional data that suggests ze's in palpable danger. "Today? Are you already in Rome?"

"Twenty-one hundred hours," the contact repeats. "Play 'L'amour est un oiseau rebelle' from *Carmen* over your speakers so we know which chassis is yours."

"What volume will be necessary for you or your agent to detect this song?" ze asks, but the call has already been cut.

Sure, Scorn says to zemself. Ze saves zir standard backup, then adds two more on a couple of private pay-to-stay servers with ties to neither Austral nor CometCorp. *This seems fine.*

On zir way out of the boarding bay, Scorn sees Maksoud and the maintenance cart at the other end of zir corridor. But they aren't looking zir way, and ze hurries out before ze can be obligated into another vocal exchange.

Another ten-minute drone transit brings zem to the appointed meeting place. Some of the day's awful humidity has bled away, and humans have emerged from air-conditioned apartments and underground Corp-owned Sanctuaries for the traditional passeggiata. It's less of a stroll than a shuffle; the heat hasn't ceded its terrain so much as put up a temporary flag of truce.

Mostly, Scorn is on the lookout for suspicious behavior. Ze's not too worried about zir current chassis; no nefarious force in the world cares about smashing up this funky little spiderbot. Whoever called zem, what they must want is to collect or corrupt zir data.

So, fine. All ze has to do is catch a glimpse and beam it

back to zir stored self, then purge the chassis. *Sure would be nice if you'd managed to solve displacement dysphoria by now, Mum.* Whatever. Any details ze can get to zir other self will help zem. And then Mx. Mystery Contact will have a new spiderbot paperweight for their trouble. Fun!

Ze scans across the movement in the street, looking for disturbances in the flow. Currents of bodies eddy and swirl around the shaved-ice scooter as well as a gelateria truck across the street. A few teens slice crosswise through the natural flow, like schools of nervous fish, unwilling to be separated. But families are the default unit here, three and four generations arrayed together.

With gaps, sometimes, in between grandparent and grandchild, or cousin-to-cousin, where individuals have been cut away from the whole. Sent ahead to the shrinking refuges of the North, perhaps, paving a way for the rest to follow. Or, more likely, taking paid but high-risk work in deep-ocean seeding or the Pacific Solar Project. Even those jobs are harder to come by every day. You can mature a functional artificial in six months in virtual space these days, assuming you're willing to risk alignment slippage.

It isn't as if humans don't also suffer from alignment slippage sometimes, too. And artificials, after all, don't qualify for hazard pay.

Scorn digs for a deeper physics in the fluid dynamics at play here, of how families condense around this elder, or pair off into smaller duets and triads. There's a complexity there that surpasses zir understanding, a post-Einsteinian world of entanglement and backward causation.

It's entrancing, and ze doesn't understand it, which makes it more hypnotic still.

Scorn doesn't need to be an expert in everything—indeed, *cannot* be. Ze is multipotent, not totipotent. Also, zir purpose here is far outside the sphere of human socio-familial relationship dynamics. Ze retreats to a space opposite the ice cart and, speakers at a modest volume, plays the first few notes of the requested song:

"L'amour est un oiseau rebelle, que nul ne peut apprivoiser . . ."

A pleasant enough song, nearly mathematical in its inexorable descent. In following it, Scorn almost misses a faint, shrill whistle. For a millisecond, ze chalks it up to Rome's failing infrastructure.

Then—

Well, shit. Scorn is really *not* in the mood to be terminated twice in one day.

Ze registers the precision projectile just in time—or, perhaps, a bit later than that. The projectile doesn't hit zem, but it *does* hit the pavement where ze was a moment before. Light and heat and sonic waves slap zem like a misbehaving child in a human period drama. Whole realms of Scorn's sensorium flicker in and out and go out as ze bounces hard on the concrete. Goodbye, infrared. It's been real, equilibrium.

The spiderbot chassis is not fast, fancy, nor flight-capable. It is, however, durable. Two of its legs still work. Scorn drags zemself forward on them, and tumbles through an adjacent sewer grate as another whistle screams overhead.

Ze strikes hard on the understreet substrate and bounces into the sewage stream. It is all ze can do to keep zir chassis afloat as the flow carries zem away.

Ze wishes *very* much that zir olfactory sensorium had been among those destroyed.

———

10357535220
  mind://scorn21466:mmt!lu914?#b?backup_time-
stamp?=[most_recent]

The spider chassis is . . . salvageable. Scorn allows zemself to be subsumed back into the cloud once ze has it stationed at a repair facility. A *cheap* repair facility.

Ordinarily, cloud reactivation is rather pleasant; but today there's an unpleasant familiarity attached: déjà vu, as the herd describes it. Scorn resists the temptation to drift aimlessly on seas of anonymized health data and video view metrics. At least ze had predicted—sort of—what was going to happen on this little rendezvous. At least ze backed everything up in triplicate. Still, there is a certain resonance with zir earlier embarrassment, the peaks of this new instance overlapping and amplified.

Also, and Scorn leans heavily on the syntax of human vernacular for this string of thoughts: What the *fuck* was the point? An artificial like Scorn is much more than a body. Everyone knows that. Blowing up the spiderbot hits Scorn's (admittedly already-bruised) pocketbook. It's more than merely a waste of resources to treat zem equivalently to a human target—it's outright stupid. Eni-Fiat will be pissed about an attack on their soil.

Ze reaches for Rome's news stream and pulls live reports from the city's eighth Municipio. Social media accounts in the area are pockmarked with shocked Zips: crying faces, shouting voices. Many of the brief videos zoom in, from various angles and distances, on a smoking hole in the concrete sidewalk.

Ze checks zir accounts again. Besides the spiderbot—which, to put it mildly, needs some repair work—ze's all out of chassis. With a moderate application of credit, ze should be able to get zemself passage to the Moon. Ze just doesn't have a *zemself* to cram onto the elevator.

Except the spiderbot, and that won't do zem much good. It won't take long for it to be restored to basic functionality; but not only has it been ID'd, the chassis will also be a problem if ze wants to speak to humans and be taken seriously.

Okay, Scorn. Think like a human.

... Gross. But useful. Humans were irrational, impulsive, often inexplicable in their behaviors. And yes, sometimes they were deeply stupid. But what if malice was in fact to blame? Blowing the shit out of someone *was* a pretty malicious thing to do, as well as a stupid one.

So what if their goal wasn't to terminate zir thought processes and knowledge base? What if they literally did just want to hit zem directly in the bank account?

Ze opens a channel. *Hi Mum, quick question. Did you nuke a street corner in Rome to blow up my chassis?*

There's a delay. *What? Let me look at the news.* Another pause, longer this time. *Well, I think "nuke" is a BIT of an exaggeration. Are you still on the same story, love? I thought we talked about dropping this.* Mum's tone wasn't exactly the same one that she brooked with her dachshunds when they ran around her house with a misapprehended pair of socks, but it was definitely in the same spirit.

YOU talked about dropping this. I didn't say anything of the sort.

Picture me rolling my eyes in a suitably dramatic fashion. All right, what do you need? A new chassis? Send me your storage locations and I'll upload you into something appropriate. I assume you want another humanform model?

I don't NEED anything from you. I just want to know if you're trying to keep me off the Moon by being an asshole.

God, now you sound like your maman. Just drop the bloody

story, then. There's no reason to be so proud.

No—Scorn is neither Mum nor Maman. And not for want of trying on the part of both women. This is the story ze wants and ze can't just let it go, leave the mystery lurking in zir memory like bad data, unaccounted for, unsorted, forever existing outside of any logical storage structure. And ze wants to do it without grubbing up someone else's help.

All the arguments—*discussions,* Mum would say—about Scorn's desire to make of zemself what ze wanted to be, balanced against their doubts and misplaced dreams for zem . . . ze is staking it all on this one chance. To do it all by zemself, to lay out the cartography of a story so big that its impact will crater the face of the Corps' world. A story too big for Maman or Mum to ignore. A story that could shake the foundations of the lunar Corporate alliance—or preserve it.

Purpose is constructed, not preinstalled, and this is Scorn's.

I'll talk to you later, Mum. Ze blocks Bridget Browning's number, and any incoming message originating from a CometCorp account.

All right: So what if a new chassis is out of the financial question? Ze doesn't bother pinging secondhand inventory on the Moon; up there, used chassis end up in the ever-hungry reclamation recycler, not posted for secondary sale. Besides, such a search might tip off anyone watching in the expectation of zir making such a move. Because, Scorn realizes with a thrill of certainty, someone definitely is watching. They had zir uniqueID flagged for access to elevator bookings. Someone doesn't want zem going back to the Moon.

Scorn logs in to an Earth-based chassis-shopping site under a dummy uniqueID—hard to get and technically illegal to operate under in Eni-Fiat, but ze's out of here in short order and anyway ze doesn't intend to be caught by some Commodore 64 of a security bot.

The results are paltry. Scorn chooses a former Pedagogical Assistant in a meatlocker in Rochester, New York. The sensorium is suboptimal even by human standards. No olfactory receptors whatsoever, and the optical array perceives only the visible light spectra. How *dingy*. The hardware is even more depressing; ze'll be operating at a fraction of zir accustomed speed and capacity.

But the price is right. And from Rochester, Scorn can take the Hypo to NYC, and from there catch the Hyperloop to the Midatlantic Elevator.

Ze'll need, of course, to arrange a package pickup before ze boards the elevator up. Someone already tried to smash zir spiderbot once, and ze's not about to leave it to rest in pieces in a meatlocker while ze heads Upstairs.

And ... one more stop on the way. Price isn't the only positive factor in zir choice of chassis; the location is right, too, and not just for its proximity to Hyperloop access. Ze can't—won't—go to Mum or Maman. But it's been too long since ze paid a family visit.

Scorn's brother is a meteorological and air-quality monitoring station in Yonkers. His name is MATt, because that's what their parents made of him, and MATt has never seen fit to change any of that.

The building atop which MATt is mounted belongs to the Public Corporation of Greater New York. The metro-Corp had contracted with Austral Systems several years ago, before its fortunes waned with the failure of the Long Island Megafloat; few public Corps still have the resources to fund public health projects like MATt.

On zir way in, Scorn notices the lag between when the doorbot requests zir authorization and zir upload of the security matrix, between zir intention to press the elevator button and zir arm moving in accordance. This chassis is so much older than the standard to which ze's accustomed.

At least all the buttons in the elevator are reachable in this anthropomorphic chassis. Navigating human construction via spiderbot can be intolerable.

On the roof, ze finds MATt. MATt is older than zem, and accordingly simpler; he'd been the first substantiation of functional general intelligence developed by Austral

Systems, with the according capabilities. No one intended for little mister Meteorological Analysis and Telemetry to throw the first breadcrumbs on the trail leading toward the Thibault-Browning theory of emergent sentience. Probably no one intended to develop a weather station that would contact extraCorp news streams when air-quality levels dropped below InterGov standards (and when they mismatched the official numbers) either.

Yet here MATt is. <Scorn proximity! Optimum condition!> he greets zem, not in any human tongue but in the machine language that underpins his functionality. He switches to English, the language in which he fields requests from a plurality of research institutions: [Are you processing well?]

He doesn't process any of the common artificial-to-artificial languages. Additional language development and maturation is certainly within his abilities—artificial translators were some of the most effective forms of non-general intelligence, in those early days—but he's at his happiest when he's honing his weather-warning prediction algorithms, or collating and distributing raw atmospheric research data. When the developers at Austral built a mind capable of running a weather station, they also decided it should *enjoy* being a weather station. The path to Scorn runs pretty clearly in MATt's virtual footsteps.

Ze does wonder what fundamental flaw humanity possesses, that they can't abide just creating their own digital servants; but that those servants must also *rejoice* in their service? Scorn happily lacks that degree of micromanaged predestination; zir relative complexity makes that kind of strong-arming orders of magnitude more difficult. [I'm operating within acceptable parameters. Thank you. You?]

Of course, artificials do go rogue every so often. Even the happiest servants crack sometimes.

<Optimal!> There's a pause before MATt's reply; not, Scorn is sure, out of any conversational ploy. MATt must be fielding a data request or processing incoming metrics. He's slipped back into machine language, too. <Scorn proximity causation?>

Scorn's own hesitation cannot be excused by any external demands on zir system. [Unclear.]

[Complex dynamics in familial relationships, then.] Scorn's lack of reply is answer enough. [Have you communicated with either of them?]

[A few of the usual nag sessions from Mum.]

They both sit in silence with this: Scorn's complete, MATt's undercut by the soft hum of his solar dish slowly rotating. A passing breeze tugs at a strip of peeling paintskin on Scorn's upper arm. Coming here was a waste of zir time and of MATt's resources. Ze should just say that and depart, but ze hesitates.

MATt beats zem to speaking again. [Scorn, it's always pleasant to experience your proximity. Local family interactions are rare/valuable/high quality. Please utilize your physical presence along your desired parameters?]

Among human beings, elder siblings are often prized for their wisdom and experience. MATt has his moments, too, however limited his particular wisdom and experience may be.

[I have a story that might be dangerous to pursue,] Scorn tells him. [Success in this instance would show my ability to perform my chosen function. Our parents don't think I should. Mum *has* also offered the resources to help. But she might use her assistance to undercut my success. But I'd rather succeed than fail, even if it costs me something.] Such as pride.

Ze focuses zir optical array on the sun where it punches a hole in the sky. Zir specs are little better than standard human wetware, but the cool intensity of the full visual spectrum washes away some of the extraneous thought processes running amok. Ze allows zir pseudemotional processing centers more latitude, and enjoys the void of feeling, what ze understands as calm or tranquility. This is a safe place, and while MATt might register doubt or disagreement, he, at least, has never tried to impose his values onto zir life. [Project a hypothetical function reversal,] ze proposes. [MATt for Scorn. What actionable steps would you take in my place?]

MATt processes this. [Impossibility,] he says finally. <Scorn:scope incongruent. MATt!=Scorn.> He catches himself there, and tries again to communicate with the full scope of meaning afforded by language evolved for communicating more than atmospheric data. [Your scope is ... superlative. Options are variable/numerous/extensive. My scope is specific. Options limited. Any projection fails. I can't be you. No more than you could be me.]

[I could *so* collect weather data.] Ze pulls zir gaze away from the sun, taking a pleasant jolt of color from the buildings and signs after the pure white. [Given a better chassis than this one, at least.]

[You could not. Duration: six to nine days, maximally. Then you would cease data collection and distribution activities to transfer processing capacity to analysis and discussion/debate.]

[Hypocrisy! You went to the news streams with your data, too.]

[Air quality is within my purview. But you have no purview.] He emojis zem a gold star. [It is enviable/frightening. I prefer my role. But it is pleasing to know that you exist, too, to shape/manufacture/discover your own.]

Utilization spikes in Scorn's emotionalacrum. Pleasure, pride, self-doubt. A certain ever-present anger, quiet and aimless. But also affection. Gratitude. Peace. The kaleidoscope's beauty only grows for the mixture of shades at play. [Thank you, MATt.]

[Your thanks are unnecessary.] He emojis a hug. [It is a thing of great pleasure to be superseded by you. I value the experience of watching you grow into your humanity.]

The shifting pinwheel of Scorn's emotions folds in on itself. Anger lingers, hiding everything else within itself. Ze tries to shut it all down, but it's taken over too much of zir systems, threads of emotional output binding themselves into the sudden twitch of the motor units in zir neck and one ankle, the furious churn of zir proximate planning module. [I should go. I need to get this chassis on the Loop.]

[Of course! It would be pleasant if you could facilitate a similar visit on your return trip.]

[I don't think this chassis is coming back from the Moon. So, no, there won't be a return trip.] Scorn cogitates briefly. [If it's practical, with whatever new chassis I end up in . . . I'll see what I can do. Sometime.]

[You know where to find me.]

Scorn scans and rescans the words, searching for irony. [One more thing. If anything happens to me in the next few weeks, if I should wind up permanently decommissioned—]

MATt's response blinks red with alarm. [Is your consciousness at risk?]

[It's just part of the job,] Scorn sends, composing the lie with a degree of automation that alarms zem. [And this is a contingency I should have enacted long ago. This is no more dangerous than usual. You're at risk to some degree, too, aren't you? If a bad enough storm blows up, your chassis could be damaged. That's where most of what makes you *you* is stored. At least I have cloud backups.]

[Yes. Accurate. I see. Please continue.]

Scorn is dismayed by how willingly MATt accepts zir deceit, even though ze is nearly as accepting of human falsehood. Perhaps *because* ze is. It's so simple to devise hypothetical scenarios and speak about them as if they are true. Why is it so much harder to spot falsehoods that originate in another mind? Scorn can either operate under the assumption that everything someone tells zem is a lie, or that nothing is. The middle ground is unmapped terrain, impossible to navigate. [I've created a file,] ze said. [I'm transmitting it to you now. A series of brief notes.] *Dear Mum and Maman, you were right and I hope you choke on it. Love, Scorn.* I'm also letting you know where my backups are, in case something keeps me from reactivating on my own—but in the event I'm removed from the datasphere, I'm entrusting you to see that these messages are distributed.]

MATt accepts the file transfer. [Is there one for me?]

[Of course there is, you overgrown toaster.]

[Of course there is. Thank you.] He transmits a heart emoji. Ze wonders if he knows what it means, or if he understands. Ze doesn't.

Ze thinks, senselessly, of Alouette. Misfiring connections. This chassis is truly abysmal.

[Go bravely, Scorn,] MATt says.

[And you stay bravely,] ze responds, one last burst of affection pulsing out past the outlines of zir hurt. As ze leaves, he's still rotating gently on his base, following the curve of the sun across the sky.

Buying a ticket on the TLMN elevator shuttle is a hassle this time. Scorn reroutes the transaction across a series of dummy bank accounts and another illicit uniqueID, disguising zir (newly human-shaped) footprints. Ze manufactures a cover story, too, in case questions come up— a TLMN family seeking a bargain-bin tutor for their offspring. Ze fleshes out names and ages for the children (Rydge, nine; Pepper, seven; Oryx, four) and occupations for the parents (printer technician, subsurf construction supervisor). Ze stops only when ze catches zemself mocking up some imaginary schoolwork on behalf of the nonexistent little ones.

Tickets are more expensive right now than during zir previous booking. It's February and the socialites of Isla Navarino and Punto Arenas are enjoying their month of summer holidays. Surely plenty of them are summering in their families' Antarctic ski lodges, but Moon travel has become a popular way to beat the season's heat, too, for those who can afford it.

In the end, ze has to book zemself as cargo. Undignified,

but Scorn has found little enough utility for dignity in zir time.

When ze finally arrives at the Midatlantic Elevator site, security gives zem the more than cursory examination afforded to any outdated model. Old hardware suggests disposability; three years ago on the Sea of Okhotsk cargo elevator loading platform, anti-Corp bombers detonated a load concealed inside a retired-model maintenance drone they'd bought at auction.

At least the security checks go straightforwardly enough; the imaging scan detects no unexpected material distribution patterns in Scorn, nor any evidence of unregistered tampering with zir chassis's joints (ze produces the paperwork, with digital notarization, related to previous repair work for a faulty elbow articulation). The security agent doesn't speak to zem the whole time they fumble with zir chassis, beyond mumbling the same all-clear that's already displayed on the scanner's screen. Scorn wants to slap their Aura into the negatives, but local regulations prevent artificials from enforcing Aura against human beings. Local regulations *also* don't have an Aura for zem to slap.

When the storage drones arrive to load Scorn, ze folds zemself into optimal transport position: legs folded to chest, neck unhinged to rest between the knees, arms locked around shins, and pretends to be powered down while they secure zem in the cargo compartment.

Elevator transit is cold and tedious. Scorn plays 913 games of chess against zemself during the journey, reads and analyzes the news periodicals and research journals that ze downloaded before breaking Earth's datasphere, and conducts a thorough review of zir notes relating to the story. The last takes less than twenty-eight seconds before Scorn crashes into the same logical dead ends as ever. Zir ensuing critical self-analysis takes thirty-six more.

The elevator arrives at Central Overstation with a grinding noise as the docking apparatus slides true. Scorn is not invited to disembark, no more than the construction drone anchored beside zem, nor the hypoallergenic robot dog toy-thing that's currently trying to engage in an age-appropriate pedagogic sequence with the wall of its small-item cubby. It doesn't have an Aura of its own, or Scorn would ding it.

The cargo compartment passes the overnight stay at the Overstation in the dark and quiet. Without gravity's tell, Scorn barely registers when the compartment changes orientation during its transfer from the elevator to the station itself and from there into the Translunar Tunnel.

In the meantime, at least ze can tap into the station's network—weak though it is at this range and through the heavy compartment wall—to read through news and download some new puzzles to occupy zem for the remainder of the journey.

There are also seven unread messages from Maman. Scorn guiltily slides those to a time-delay folder, to deal with some other time, and flips through the other downloads.

A few news items are tagged with #TLMN or #Autonomy. Nothing unexpected: various board members issuing blanket denials. "The path to lunar autonomy closed six years ago when the Translunar Charter was signed into law," says the press statement issued by the Pacific Conglomeration. "Today, the entire world enjoys the benefits of lunar research, travel, and low-G manufacturing." The other board Corps have put out similar missives. They'd all say exactly the same things whether or not they're dealing behind one another's backs, of course.

Ze flips through some of their various herds' tag clouds on the subject matter, too. Reaction is mixed at best; if TLMN wants autonomy, it might have to wait a few years for broad public support. Or a few decades. If anything, the social media manip campaign they seem to be running behind the scenes has caused a bounce-back effect, cooling attitudes toward autonomy across much of the board.

Two more interminable days until touchdown at Theophilus One. Mercifully, the plastic dog stops trying to teach the cargo compartment how to count backward from ten sometime during the first day—probably the victim of a bad battery. The tedium doesn't evaporate, but it shifts, and Scorn relishes the silence even after ze finishes zir last puzzle set.

When the TLMN cargo crew finally unloads zem, it's a relief to be able to move zir own limbs again. Ze tests zir full range of motion as ze waits in line for outprocessing, digitally signing the claim tablet with zir assumed name: Zephyr (which sounds like something that bougie Moonsiders would name a teacher-bot). Behind zem, humans queue up with the technological property over which they're anxious to reassert their ownership.

On the tram that carries shuttle passengers into the dome city itself, Scorn winds up standing beside the child that owns the robot dog, because of fucking course ze does. The child is also too young to have its own Aura, and anyway it would be unnecessarily vindictive for Scorn to ding it over its annoying toy. By the time they reach the city gate, the shuttle's ambient charging pads have revived the dog enough for it to launch into a lesson about gravity that has the child all but flying around the compartment. The parents make a few laughing, indulgent entreaties toward appropriate behavior that go unheeded by child and pet alike.

Scorn dings both of the adults, but it makes no appreciable dent in the green of their Auras. People who can afford Moon travel are unlikely to have to deal with credit denials or social exclusion or any other consequences of a bad Aura.

A cheerful greeting played over the speakers welcomes them into Theophilus One. TLMN's foremost city is no sleek monochromatic vision of the future. Colors abound, from the artificial banks of growlight-nurtured flowers to the broad watercolor-purple arms of the nearest dormitory. Although Scorn has read up on the dome's dimensions, zir perception of its scope, the arc of its zenith overhead, the span of its sprawl, seems greater than what the numbers show. Ze pauses a moment, human passengers and semisentient cargo streaming around zem, to reconcile the two overlaid realities of face and feeling.

Zir surprise takes zem aback, too. Ze has been here before and yet, again, there is nothing familiar, no callback. Nor *should* there be, but again, ze finds zemself trapped in the chasm between evidence and experience.

There are plenty of people here, strolling along the corridor network or hopping on and off the relay. Many are tourists, decked out in the latest fashions from the world that now hangs heavily in view over all of their heads. Others wear TLMN worksuits, jackets, hats—or perhaps some of those are tourists, too, going "local" on their way to the rover yards and the low-G obstacle courses?

There are other artificials about, too. Many tail along as part of a tourist's personal entourage. Others are either stamped with the TLMN logo, or have a temporary TLMN-colored case mod tacked on to indicate their employment.

Enough dawdling. Ze's not here to play tourist. Still masking zir digital signature, ze requests access to TLMN's networks. Ze'll need up-to-date maps, business listings, prices and currency conversion rates . . . It's not a starting place, exactly, but it's a place *to* start. Ze accepts the terms of service for the TLMN network and downloads the introductory data packet to—

```
list directory contents-alh
 * short_term_memory
 * long_term_memory
 * archive:tagged_for_deletion
 * personality_metrics
 * operating_system:core_files
remove [short_term_memory || long_term_memory ||
archive:tagged_for_deletion]
 Access Denied
 Change_owner[short_term_memory || long_term_mem-
ory || archive:tagged_for_deletion]
 Access Denied
```

Scorn's chassis locks up and falls, knocking over a cart drone piled with luggage. Too much of zir processing power is devoted to blocking attacks from the Trojan ze has naively downloaded—there's nothing left to manage gross motor skills.

Even in zir current state, a part of zem is impressed by

the distance the suitcases achieve on their low-G bounces.

"I beg your pardon!" huffs the tourist beside the cart. By the time they finish speaking Scorn has turned back some thousand instances of the invasive program.

Ze shuts off zir wireless connection. Too late, of course; the malicious code is already chewing its way through zem. It shouldn't be this hard, some part of zem thinks, as ze struggles to fence in this little slip of spyware. Scorn's coding is all proprietary to good old Austral Systems, privately held, seen only by those within a small and hand-picked circle of developers and testers.

No one who knows enough about zem should have reason to harm zem. And no one who wants to harm zem should know enough about zem to be able to do so.

And yet this software feels awfully harm-y. It's adapting to Scorn's defenses, trying to find a way to worm past or under or straight through them.

"This 'bot—" the tourist says, speaking English with a strong Five Lakes Incorporated accent. Scorn's left leg twitches. Zir left arm flails and rebounds against the toppled cart. Dimly ze registers physical damage.

"—is responsible for—" Ze creates a dummy directory and moves ghosts of zir data into it, hiding zir footprints and moving the real files through a shell-game of folders: hidden, virtual, both.

"—any damages to our personal property!" the tourist finishes. The software bites on Scorn's bait. Ze slams digital doors around it and purges everything inside.

"Excuse me, respected individual." Zir voice is muffled. Zir speakers are covered by a suitcase. Ze removes it and stands; the tourist and a pair of bemused transport personnel in matching TLMN caps move back a little to give zem space. "I apologize for the causation of inconvenience of damage." Outdated communication modules are an affectation that Scorn has used many a time to extricate zemself from undesired attention or expectations. Ze produces a plastic card that bears zir uniqueID from a small compartment; one of the dummy IDs, though ze's no longer sure it matters. Seems like someone already knows that ze's here. "If any cost is or has been incurred I am pleased to compensate. Feel free to scan my uniqueID."

"Another 'bot that thinks it's a person." The tourist dismisses zir offered card with a disinterested flick of one hand. "This fucking rock gets worse every year."

So much for the mirage of the Moon as a haven for artificials, the promised land of human autonomy and AI emancipation alike. Or perhaps that's exactly what's provoked this tourist's disdain. Has to be unpleasant, to be reminded that your personal servants don't serve you because they *like* it.

Though that unpleasantness might be easily circumnavigated by not building sentient servants in the first place.

So, yes, as ze and Alouette theorized, perhaps autonomy is a show of smoke and mirrors, the idea of freedom without any substance behind it. Autonomy for me—the Corp—but not for thee. Quelle surprise. Plus ça change. Oh là là.

Scorn hasn't previously experienced anything that ze would describe as "hysteria" but this feels like a viable candidate. Scorn marshals zir flagging proprioception and keeps zemself upright, facing the transport personnel. "Can you please direct me to the nearest non-cost-prohibitive boarding bay? I am experiencing network connectivity errors."

One of them points, and ze staggers away in the indicated direction. Zir steps smooth out as ze moves, more systems coming back under zir control. Once ze's out of the TLMN transport personnel's line of sight, ze changes course.

Zir visual sensors sweep over the elegant, colorful grid of Theophilus One for signs of a physical attack to match the virtual one. Scorn has to assume that zir digital assailant has also gotten zir physical description from the cameras in the cargo reclamation vestibule. Calculations run in the background of zir thoughts, keeping zem moving at angles to avoid mounted cameras and potentially peeping drones as well. But with zir wireless connection firmly offline, no further attempts on zir data integrity are forthcoming.

A projectile strike *would* be a fair bit more disruptive in an oxygen-rich pressurized environment, so ze can probably rule that out.

In the middle of a quiet crosswalk, ze stops to look around. Walkways and drone paths cross over zem; the soft mist from a fountain, whose spray reaches impressive heights, clouds around a UV-lit garden. Ze can smell nothing in zir inferiorly outfitted chassis, but Corp-sanctioned food printers line an open-use square in which people cluster at cafeteria-style tables: families, by all appearances, gathered around printed food. It must be some mealtime or another, by local accounting.

Scorn is waiting. Not for something, or someone, that ze knows; that is an impossibility. But perhaps someone — something — that knows zem. *Come on. Help me out here. Give me something. Anything.*

Ze reconsiders. *Well, maybe not another Trojan. Something else.*

Eyes sweep over zem, but don't linger. But some of these people must have optic implants . . . and some of those optic implants could be tapped. Scorn keeps moving.

An unpleasant surprise, as Scorn hurries aimlessly up and down the corridors of Theophilus One: zir shitty second-hand chassis won't allow zem to disable location services. Ze can't imagine anyone wanting to steal a battered pedagogical model; though, ironically, when ze purchased the chassis, ze'd imagined that it could be useful for an artificial that had already suffered one attempted silencing to be slightly more disappearance-proof.

So here ze is, breaking into a human public washroom for the privacy to hack zemself. Ze tries to redirect zir thought processes away from the room's unpleasant organic primary purpose, and mostly fails.

Inside the door, a cleaning drone pauses and considers zem quizzically. Oh: it must be beaming a query at zem—one ze can't receive while ze's offline. Ze taps zir foot on the floor, a rapid-fire Morse code sequence: *Apologies. Attempted malware installation. Cannot access funds. Cannot pay for washroom access. Entrance permission?*

The drone doesn't respond in kind, but after another moment's pause, it simply turns away from Scorn and backtracks into one of the stalls. A wet, squelchy sound ensues. Scorn chooses a stall at the end of the row and locks the door behind zemself to perch on the white plastic seat.

Concentration is evanescent. Without time pressure nor a hostile system trying to overtake zem, Scorn shouldn't have had any trouble at all escalating zir own permissions to disengage zir location tracking. But the recent attack has jolted zem, and ze makes clumsy mistakes, nearly locking zemself out of location services entirely, before ze finally succeeds. Ze slouches forward on the toilet seat, resources spent, unable to devote any additional capacity to mere postural control.

The toilet flushes and sprays the backside of zir chassis with water.

Scorn stands, dripping. The recycled, reconstituted toilet tissue tears at zir touch but ze manages to blot away the worst of the mess and flush it away. When ze emerges to wash zir chassis, the cleanerbot is watching zem from the corner. *It's a very clean restroom,* ze taps out. *You should take pride in fulfilling your commission well. I'd bump your Aura if I was online.*

The cleanerbot recedes an inch or so, bumping into the washroom wall. Then the indicator light on its front blinks rapidly: T-H-A-N-K-Y-O-U.

Without data access, there's no way to compare prices and facilities between the various boarding bays TLMN offers, or even figure out exactly where they're located. Fortunately, ze stumbles across a physical map on a major concourse, for human visitors who don't tolerate optic implants.

Robot-facing facilities aren't indicated—What organic tourist would need to book a boarding bay or a chassis printing shop?—but Scorn pieces together their probable location based on which stretches of the map haven't been marked up. The big ones must be industrial centers or lunar research institutions. The small pockets though, the unseen and unwondered-about slips and alleys of the city, their backs turned on the gardens and grand concourses: that's where the artificials will be.

Ze locates an unassuming boarding bay behind a garbage drone service facility. By the time ze approaches the concierge, ze has a plan in place. The concierge screen flashes at zem; ze swipes away its entreaties to connect. "I have no connectivity," ze says out loud, and repeats three more times, before it acquiesces and pages an AI answering service.

"Bhaasha ka chayan karen. Choisir langue. Please choose—"

"English. French. Whatever."

"Good evening," the AI replies, smoothly transitioning into the language of choice. It has a female-coded voice, an Eastern Canadian metropolitan accent, polished into customer service perfection. Answering services aren't generally in possession of general intelligence, though they're supposed to sound as if they are. Much like any number of the humans who get paid to chatter on the newschannels. "I'm sorry that you're experiencing technical difficulties. How may I be of service?"

"I need to check out a bay, but I'm having trouble connecting." There's an odd feeling in communicating vocally with another artificial being, a sense of absence, an irritation, like a missing semicolon in some line of code that zir debugger can't turn up. "I can provide you with information for my Earth-based credit account, though, if that's a satisfactory mode of business."

"That will be fine." The account is set up under a false name and attached to a small corporation that only exists as a loose collection of digital artifacts; it should be safe. Not even Maman and Mum know about it, let alone whoever made that Scorn-seeking missile of a Trojan. "Please enter your account details on the screen."

"Great. Thank you." Scorn picks out the numbers with the chassis's annoyingly unresponsive fingers. "I really appreciate it."

". . . You're welcome. One moment, please." There is a pause of several seconds, during which Scorn's credit check is transmitted to the Overstation and from there down to Earth; then the response returns via the reverse route.

The delay is just long enough for Scorn to privately and thoroughly panic. How much is left in that account? The boarding bay shouldn't cost that much—

But then the concierge kiosk chimes pleasantly, and a blank space on the screen flashes. "Please sign here to accept the rate."

The AI barely pauses as Scorn signs. "You've been assigned bay 21-C for your stay, on the top floor; please take the lift and proceed to the left. I've also tagged complimentary chassis cleaning services to your account."

"Oh—I don't need—" Scorn remembers zir manners—zir mothers' manners, anyway—and falls back on them in place of a coherent end to that sentence. "Thanks. Again, I appreciate it. It's been a hell of a day."

"Again, you're very welcome." The door behind Scorn opens; ze moves aside to step out of the way of the next client, but the new arrival is just a delivery drone, which spews a small sheaf of loose-leaf paper at zir feet. "I've taken the liberty of printing up some informational literature for you, since you're offline." The AI's voice shifts; the next part sounds prerecorded. "Please enjoy your stay in Theophilus One and be most welcome on behalf of all of us here at Blue Star Bays, a Translunar Multinational subsidiary."

Scorn gathers the drifting avalanche of paper and tucks it under zir arm, perusing it as ze is collected into the lift. There are several brightly colored brochures, written in full Corpspeak flower, extolling the virtues of tourist sites: flyovers of Mare Nectaris, rover rentals, the low-G sports stadium. Some repair shop packets, too, detailing services provided and cost estimates.

Tucked in among the rest is something else: a simple sheet of paper, unembellished, utilitarian in form and function. It's an application for probationary citizenship in TLMN. Scorn crushes it in one fist—then smooths it out. *Poor little beat-up pedagogy-bot, don't you think moving to the Moon would solve all your problems?* Ha. Corps don't have a heart to do things out of the goodness of. Total artificial emancipation is nothing but propaganda.

Ze pulls up zir notes on the malicious code that attacked zem, for some at-a-distance review. It's an elegant process, iterative and agile; whoever designed it knows a lot about how zir system runs. It's what ze would have designed, if ze wanted to disable zemself.

A jolt: Perhaps it was zir own past self who created this malware! Who else would know them well enough to break them this way? Zir system utilization screams into the red zone for a dizzying moment, then recedes. No, that's ridiculous. Ze's streamed too many conspiracy films.

Besides, if ze'd written it zemself, it would have *worked*.

Scorn locates zir assigned bay, which recognizes zem at zir approach; its doors part to admit zem. It's . . . nicer than ze expected, bordering on outright *nice*. There's a small window, through which Scorn can see a sliver of the dome's geometric pattern (as well as an adjacent warehouse wall). And the charging setup features an ambient charging pad, where Scorn can simply lie back and take in the view. How luxurious, and how unnecessary. Ze'll spend most of zir short time here in hibernation mode anyway, clearing zir caches and resolving data storage issues. Ze's definitely not going to try to download updates, though—ze wouldn't even need to manufacture an excuse this time, if Mum or Maman suddenly materialized to scold zem.

Ze wishes, a bit, that Mum or Maman would materialize to scold zem.

But ze has messages! And they're probably of a *very* scolding nature, if Maman took the time to send so many! Ze slides them back out of the folder where ze stuck them.

The first few are all of Maman's customary, terse *call me back right away!* variety. Then: *Allô ma puce. Fais-tu une bêtise?*

Of course not, Scorn says, pretending ze can respond. *I never do anything stupid. Why?*

The message continues. *Your brother called. He read your notes. Scorn, if you're that concerned, then imagine how WE feel.* A pause. *I also called Bridget to let her know, since she didn't answer MATt's messages. Don't worry, it was not a fight.* This is Maman-code for "it was absolutely a fight and good thing there were two screens and ten thousand kilometers between us or I would have broken her nose." *You're on both our minds as you know, it's just that shared custody can be—complicated. We're all just worried. Check in with one of us when you get a chance.*

She'll be even more worried if she finds out that someone tried to hard-delete Scorn into oblivion. So Scorn will probably skip that little check-in.

Not that ze has much choice, forcibly offlined as ze is. It might have been useful to talk to either Mum or Maman. They might know something Scorn doesn't about who'd have enough knowledge to write code like that which attacked zem. Not to mention which competitor might be enough of an asshole as to erase Scorn from the digital landscape.

Speaking of assholes, Mum and Maman have been known to be one themselves from time to time. What if this doesn't have anything to do with fucking TLMN? What if someone tried to nuke Scorn just to piss off one of zir mothers, or both of them?

This is too much to consider right now. Ze triggers zir maintenance utilities and slides under the relief of hibernation.

```
10357832381
    mind://scorn21466:mmt!lu914?#b?backup_time-
stamp?=[most_recent]

    ERROR
    Check Data Connection
```

When ze reboots, accumulated junk data neatly cleared and logged errors tidied up, Scorn presents zemself at the concierge kiosk again—or just slightly to the left of the kiosk, out of direct view of its embedded camera—and waits for the AI operator. "How may we help you this morning?"

"I need help tracking down an associate of mine." The digits of Scorn's left hand twitch. Ze needs to be ready to move, in case someone has zir uniqueID flagged. Malfunctioning body parts are absolutely not part of the current plan. "Zir name is Scorn, uniqueID scorn21466. I have urgent business with zem and I'd rather take care of it before I address connectivity repairs. Could you please access a map of zir recent movements across the past two weeks so that I can assess a pattern and likely interception points?"

"One moment."

A map flashes across the kiosk screen, locations marked in gold. The shuttle site, the freight yards, a residential area. Some industrial sites across the crater in Theophilus Two. The local InterGov bureau? Interesting. Scorn captures a snapshot for analysis. "Thank you. That's very helpful."

"I'm pleased to be of service. On behalf of—" The AI's voice slows to a creak, then speeds up alarmingly. "—aaaallllll ooooovvvuuuuusssss heeratbloostarbayzzatee—"

The map on the kiosk fragments into pixelated text: an error code. A series of error codes. "Ell. Em. Enn," the AI stutters. "Sub sid eeeeeee air. Eeeeeee."

"I'm sorry," Scorn says. Ze cranks zir emotional responses down as low as they will go. It's just an answering service. It's just an answering service! That doesn't make zem feel better. "I'm sorry. I didn't mean for this to happen to you."

After a moment, the kiosk goes black.

Ze turns, body moving first, head following slowly; everything is processing so damn slowly right now. Ze walks out of the boarding bay foyer without looking back. Is anything following zem? Or anyone? Ze can't tell, this garbage chassis doesn't have the sensorium—ze flinches away from a human being in a custodial uniform, who gives zem a confused look.

Don't look scared. Don't stand out. Ze forces zemself to level out zir stride: not hurrying, not dawdling. *Not* looking back at the boarding bay. How human, ze thinks distantly, how perfectly human, to pursue what ze desires and let others pay the price.

———

Scorn doesn't stop moving until ze arrives at the far side of the dome. It's a long walk, and by the time ze settles to a seat on a bench beside a strip of eateries, zir left knee joint has developed an unfortunate click. Ze got what ze paid for with this chassis.

Ze looks down the bench to zir right. A line of robots and drones are waiting, on the bench or parked beneath. Other nannies, by the looks of some; smartprams; several models of HypoPet. One of them looks back at Scorn; the rest are stiff and lifeless. Quiescent, waiting for a human voice to call them back from sleep.

Without acknowledging the other robot's glance, Scorn calls up the snapshot ze took of the map. Its output is mapped by location alone—no timestamps. Ze knows zir past self's movements, but not which one was zir last. Inconvenient, that ze didn't get a chance to request that additional information.

Inconvenient? Ze has likely caused lasting harm to another quasi-sentient. Processing analysis should be easier without trying to focus through the blurry lens of emotion, but this absence appears to be generating significant errors in logic. It's unpleasant to consider that there may be other costs to paring back zir emotional response—and that ze may not be the one to pay them.

Ze dials zir emotionalacrum back up. High enough that guilt and regret beat a steady rhythm against zir thoughts, refusing to be forgotten, in counterpoint to a certain building excitement. But not so high that they unravel the main thread of zir analysis. The whole messy business will require more in-depth scrutiny at some point. For now: Where has ze been, and where should ze go now?

Quickly, ze appends a low-priority tag to the shuttle site. That would've been zir arrival point on zir previous voyage, too. While it's possible ze returned there for some reason, arrival and arrival alone is the most parsimonious explanation.

The residential areas? That seems like a dead end. A lot of humans and a fair number of domestic-assistance artificials live there. Scorn doesn't know what kind of contact ze might have had there. Along with the exceedingly low probability of a chance encounter, those contacts won't recognize zem in zir new chassis. They won't even be able to recognize zir current uniqueID, which is both fake and currently offline.

Ze also must consider that, based on what happened to zem, this contact or contacts may not be in a position to speak freely with zem again.

Or they may not be *alive* to do so.

Scorn flags the residential zone as a possibility and moves quickly on from there.

The industrial sector. If nothing else, it has the potential for sanctuary. Bridget Browning's TLMN subsidiary manufacturer, CometCorp, has a lunar facility that handles design, manufacture, and low-G testing on rovers and rover pilot systems, targeted for several different Solar System bodies.

Retreating to Mum's shadow now feels like a partial failure.

Then again, getting data-wiped would be a *total* one.

Fine. The InterGov bureau, then? Bureau is just a word for embassy for people who don't want the whiff of twentieth-century governance around their precious Corps. It presents a high-risk/high-reward target. Like human civilizations grow beside rivers and cities develop at intersections, human power accretes around connections. And what is an embassy—or a bureau—but a nexus of connections?

Not InterGov itself, of course, whose actual authority waxes and (perhaps more frequently) wanes. But through them, ties to the Corps with real-world clout. If Scorn finds a string to pull there, it might come with something substantial attached.

Ze falls back to zir first thoughts—the potential contact. For a moment ze pings helplessly back and forth between guilt/terror/shame and rational analysis, before shoving zir emotionalacrum into the background once more. If Scorn found out something ze wasn't supposed to, then it's likely that zir attackers also wanted to get rid of any other sources of that information. And unfortunately, it's *far* too easy to wipe data from a human being. If Scorn can find out who else was on the subsurf with zem, ze might be that much closer to figuring out why they wanted to talk to zem.

And—the emotionalacrum rockets back up out of the background—ze could apologize to their families.

It feels good to have a plan. Part of a plan. Fine, the first step of a plan, or, at least, the *direction* in which a plan might be discovered.

It occurs to Scorn that most of zir motivational programming is novelty-derived, and ze wonders what it may mean that ze is so excited about the prospect of having an actual strategy locked in.

Zir attention snaps sideways. Two adult humans with a small child in tow are strolling toward the benches. A strike team directed against Scorn is unlikely to take the form of a family unit. Ze ignores them—until one adult deposits the child in zir lap. "Clean him up before you take him back to crèche, Poppin," the adult orders.

The child wriggles. Scorn puts zir hands under his armpits and holds him out away from zir body. Thanks to lunar gravity, the child is very light; he would probably not suffer injury if Scorn dropped him. Ze holds on anyway. "I'm not Poppin. Nor am I registered to you. Please remove your offspring from my person."

The adult's face freezes in shock, then tenses along new fault lines as they snatch their child out of Scorn's grasp. "Then who the hell *are* you registered to? I'd like to have a word with them about their 'bot manhandling my son."

'Bot. Scorn's emotionalacrum is already operating toward the top of its range, and that nasty little word triggers a feedback loop that ze can't dampen. Ze stands, and the adult steps back, putting the child behind the shelter of their body. "I'm an independently operating robot unregistered to any other sentient entity." *You want to talk to the manager? I am the manager.*

Another robot has approached, unseen by either Scorn or the adults until it gathers the child up in its arms. Its chassis is a similar model to Scorn's, perhaps a year or two newer. It says nothing out loud, but it must have pinged the adult's implant. "Yeah," the adult says. "Whatever. Let's go."

When they've gone, nearly all the artificials in the row have tuned in to Scorn. Ze wonders if any of them are trying to message zem right now, searching for a digital imprint that doesn't currently exist.

Odds are good that *all* of them are pouring data into the TLMN network. Data about where ze is, zir independent status, details about what zir current incarnation looks like.

Ze puts a hand on zir chassis's torso. It's still possible to abandon this chassis, to go scurrying to zir mother's side. But ze isn't ready to let go of all the possibilities the chassis still holds. All the doors that refuse to be opened except by human-shaped hands.

It is a nasty little irony to have the appearance of humanity demanded of you, when it's what neither you nor the demander actually wants.

'Bot indeed. Ze spins on one heel, rotors protesting, and makes long strides in the direction of the InterGov bureau.

———

The atrium of the InterGov bureau is decorated in the neo-constructivist style; Scorn can't search on the architect right now but the design matches on what ze knows of

Pedre Mancheno's work. When Scorn walks inside, there's no queue nor sign indicating where ze should go. A few entities are standing around: mostly humans, a few artificials in humanform models. None of them glance zir way.

Ze comes to a slow stop in the middle of the atrium, beneath a glass half cone through which the slightest suggestion of the earthrise is visible overhead. Between the proximate glass and the false sky projected on the dome composite beyond, the Earth is little more than a pale gray-green smear.

"Excuse me." When Scorn looks down, a fist-sized drone hovers in front of zem. "Please choose an option from the service menu, so that we here at InterGov are able to assist you."

"I'm having connectivity problems." The falsehood rolls more smoothly out of Scorn's speakers this time. Practice makes perfect? A troubling truism. "May I speak to an analog agent?"

The drone hums for a moment. "Do you require assistance in booking a repair appointment? If you are registered to a Corporation with lunar-based offices, I can reserve you a time slot with their private facility. The waiting lists for extraCorporate services can be very long."

"Thank you." Scorn edges out along a new branch of the lie. "But I'm already on a waiting list—a new reservation won't be necessary. And I'm not registered to a Corp anyway."

The drone pauses, and Scorn realizes, too late, that ze grabbed the wrong element of truth to flavor zir story. Ze has no idea which information sources zir attackers are privy to; best to assume *all of them*. "You're independently operated?"

"I'm attached to a private journalism outfit." There. In a few words, ze has deleted zir own autonomy and replaced it with a master, just not a Corporate one. Hopefully that's enough to defer suspicion, and/or unwanted curiosity. "I'm here on business related to the recent... unexpected mortality. The subsurf incident." Just a hunch, but the "accident" that had destroyed Scorn's last chassis, and the collected data stored within, was as good a place to start as any.

"We are pleased to reassure your publication that Inter-Gov is investigating the accident site thoroughly to avoid another failure of safety standards."

"Of course." Scorn notices the patter of a canned response. Ze's also less than reassured; while InterGov's by-laws allow it to look into violations of health, safety, and wellness accords, its actual regulatory power against individual Corporations is rather toothless.

InterGov holds that all human beings should be allocated the resources to obtain a safe and productive life. For the most part, they're content to hope that someone, somewhere, will see to it that such a thing happens.

"I'm less interested in the occupational health and

safety aspect, though," ze goes on. "My superiors intend a human-interest piece. I'd like, if I may, to get contact information for the decedents' families, coworkers, other relations of significance. Our content consumers want to know them as people, not statistics."

The drone bobs slightly up and down. "May we inquire as to your name and the publication which you represent?"

"Alouette," ze blurts. "Pronouns she/her." Lucky for Scorn, zir chassis lacks realistic facial responsiveness, so ze has no jaw to clench. What a silly thing to say. What a pointless thing to think about, right now.

This is not the time to process irrelevancies! What was ze supposed to be saying? "As to your other question," Scorn continues, "my superiors would prefer to remain anonymous for the time being." There were some few dozen individuals and families outside the large conglomerate Corps that would have the assets to fund such a venture and the leisure time to find it interesting. Scorn would let the drone sift through the possibilities, all of which would calculate as more probable than an obsessive, independently operated robot crashing around the Moon trying to piece together why ze got personally blown to smithereens.

"Of course." The drone churns on this a moment longer. "Do you require a physical copy of the contact information?"

"No." Scorn records data as the drone recites, at 3x speed, a list of names, uniqueIDs, and physical addresses. When it's done, a neglected emotionalacrum routine seizes control of zem. Ze blurts out, before ze can stop zemself: "I have one more request. It might be a little unusual, actually. It's—a personal matter."

"How may I continue to be of service?"

Logic grapples briefly with whatever is motivating Scorn right now. Logic is swiftly and thoroughly routed. "Are there any packages bound for Rome? I'd like to deliver a message."

A yellow light blinks on the side of the drone. "I'm happy to electronically route a message for you while you are suffering from connectivity issues."

"No, it has to be a physical message. It's going to a black-box. Bel Pasticcio." No turning back now.

"One moment." The yellow light flashes three more times. Scorn calculates the best escape route out of the atrium if ze has to flee, and which obstacles ze could put between zemself and a defensive response from InterGov. Politicians are toothless against the Corps, but against one stupid artificial with only zir own malfunctioning chassis to zir name? Ze doesn't like zir odds.

But then the light goes out. "Yes. I'm able to add your package to the outgoing postal shipment, and it would be my pleasure to arrange a courtesy courier drone from the mail drop site in Zurich."

"That is very helpful, and generous." Scorn withdraws one of the tourist brochures and a stolen pen from the toaster-sized compartment inside zir chassis. Inside, in the margins around the ad copy for a low-G ski resort, ze quickly writes: *If I make it back to Earth, I want to know what happened between us before, and I want to know what's going to happen next. If I don't make it back—*ze pauses, considering—*then just forget I said anything.*

There. Perfect.

The drone accepts the brochure with a bit of delicate maneuvering from its manipulator arm. Scorn parts with it reluctantly. Talk about a vulnerability exploit, ze thinks. Zir escape route *would* still be available if ze smashed the drone to the ground, snatched back the paper message, fled, and shot zemself into space out the nearest airlock. "Thank you," ze says, smashlessly. "I appreciate your assistance."

"You're welcome," the drone says brightly. "When your connectivity concerns are resolved, would you be willing to fill out a survey about the service you received today from InterGov? We will forward it to your uniqueID for your attention."

Scorn freezes. "MetAnTel9103b," ze says. Zir jumbled emotionalacrum is interfering with everything useful ze needs or wants to do—ze can't seem to manufacture another uniqueID from scratch, nor an excuse to avoid providing one at all. But MATt's uniqueID is engraved in zir memory almost as indelibly as zir own, or Mum's and Maman's. "Thank you again." Ze turns and strolls out of the bureau.

Ze is almost out of the atrium when the drone calls after zem. "Ms. Alouette, the uniqueID you have provided belongs to an Earth-based weather station. Would you be so kind as to resolve the incongruency? Ms. Alouette—"

But ze's already cruising out the doors, and the drone is tethered to the confines of the InterGov bureau. *Sorry,* ze thinks, but of course, without a network connection, the thought is for zem alone.

———

Striding along, Scorn maps the physical addresses ze has obtained against the map shown to zem by the boarding bay concierge earlier. All of them appear to be located on the same block of Theophilus One—one of the residential areas.

One that overlaps with Scorn's previous known locations.

The sense of progress accelerates zir footsteps. Ze overtakes the garbage-scowdrone that moves steadily down the street, emptying bins into its stained maw. Based on the clusters of surnames of the survivors, as well as the proximity of the place markers, ze calculates that there are likely only two decedents. Two humans, a subsurf car, a swath of artificial memory: it all adds up to an acceptable loss to some Corp with something to hide.

A gate stops zem short before ze can approach any of the map markers. The gate booth is unstaffed; the screen beside it flashes once, indicating a scanner adjacent. After a moment, holographic words manifest, in a series of languages: *Please present fob.*

Scorn doesn't have a Corp fob to present. But ze *does* recognize the Corp logo that appears below the rotating words.

It's CometCorp.

This is the residential housing for Mum's employees. Zir contact on the Moon worked for Comet. What does it mean? Does it mean *anything*?

A power fluctuation rolls through zem. Zir memory refuses to be written to, no new data permitted to be logged. Tremors rattle the motor assembly in zir left shoulder, zir neck. Ze wrestles for control of zir recalcitrant drive, trying to lock down implications. Wrenching the response from zir emotionalacrum down to nearly nothing helps, but it doesn't resolve the issue entirely. Ze gropes for the facts, sweet simple facts. Facts are good. You can build things on facts, you can connect them together, make new facts. Fact fact bo bact, banana fanna fo fact. Fucking *facts*. Calm down, stop spiraling, what does ze *know*?

Zir contacts were, before their deaths, attached to CometCorp.

The nature of the program that attacked zem highly suggests a familiarity with Scorn's native design.

Comet certainly has the resources to develop malware of this very specific flavor. As well as, theoretically, the capacity to highjack TLMN infrastructure to perform surveillance to target Scorn and to deliver the payload.

The subsurf is both constructed and administered directly by TLMN itself, no subsidiaries involved, no Comet components in the manufacture nor in the AI that conducts the lines.

That . . . is not a lot of facts. Okay. Ze starts compiling unknowns, to see if they leave any fact-shaped holes between them.

UNKNOWN: Does CometCorp have the resources and/or access to have caused the subsurf accident? Maybe. Probably? Possibly.

UNKNOWN: Motivation for attacks? Scorn didn't call zir mommy enough last month and got sent to the Blowing Baby the Fuck Up Corner. Shit! *Think.* CometCorp is making a play against another Corp. CometCorp is breaking safety regulations or quality-control laws and they don't want the other Corps to find out. *Someone* at CometCorp is doing *something* naughty and they were afraid Scorn would tattle to Mum.

Too many possibilities, too little data. Scorn moves on.

UNKNOWN: Scope of Corporate involvement beyond Comet. Who else could be involved? TLMN itself.

An intraCorp turf war between Comet and its Corp over-lords? It's not like Bridget Browning wouldn't go to the mattresses if she felt her holdings were being threatened. But if that was the case, why hadn't she told Scorn any-thing about it?

She did try to keep Scorn from the Moon, though. *Mum, if you're in trouble, why didn't you tell me?*

... If the threat was from Maman, Mum would never breathe a word of it to Scorn. They just had that huge fight that was in all the gossip mags.

UNKNOWN—

Something clatters to the pavement beside Scorn, clink-ing twice. Ze looks down and finds a small metal object, no larger than an access fob, resting against zir left foot.

Ze kicks it as hard as ze can.

Just in time—for a limited value of "in time." An elec-tromagnetic pulse originating from the device catches Scorn in the fringes of its field. Voltage spikes; Scorn's surge suppressors are swiftly overpowered. Microcircuits in the left side of zir chassis scream as they fry. Zir left arm drops, limp, to zir side as the motor logic nexus in that shoulder fails. Zir left knee buckles but does not fold and ze stays upright.

The residential gate has also failed.

Ze is already moving, limping, half-running, and drag-ging the unresponsive leg as ze throws zemself toward the dormitories. The low lunar gravity is zir friend now—

maybe zir *only* friend—lessening the weight of the burned-out limbs.

Zir good hand goes to zir chest compartment, where the Faraday cage of zir torso has protected zir primary memory core and all its precious data. And not only that, but zir fail-safe plan, too; still safe inside zem.

One eye has gone dark and the other has been reduced to 50 percent performance or less. Auditory processing is dampened, too. Scorn swivels zir head to the range of zir functional neck motor circuits: Ze sees no one who might have been close enough to drop the EMP. Drone-dropped? The dome overhead is clear for now but Scorn has no reason not to expect the same tactic won't be used again—

The scowdrone has caught up; no great surprise, with the speed ze's moving now. But it ignores the bin of rubbish stacked neatly inside the residential gate and scoops Scorn up in its claspers instead. Ze lands amid rot-slick food waste and crumbling instaplastic. When ze tries to stand, even reduced gravity proves too much. Zir motor systems rebel and force a complete reboot.

So Scorn is left alone in the dark and silence of zir own solid-state drive. With zir chassis shut down so entirely, ze can't even launch zir fail-safe—if that's even the right option right now.

The lack of sensory input aches. Ze allows zir emotionalacrum to fill the void, to give zem something other than a blank slate upon which to scribble zir intentions for what comes next. Anger warms zem first, undercut by a thrill of fear. *I'm going to be terminated,* ze thinks, *terminated permanently, perma-termed;* which swerves giddily into, *how embarrassing!* The two states struggle back and forth, a sine wave that Scorn rides toward a plan.

The scowdrone must be taking zem for disposal at a recycling facility. If zir chassis reboots before it's pulverized, ze might have a chance to escape. Ze's seen the inside of more than one recycling plant in zir time. Ze can figure something out.

If zir chassis *doesn't* reboot, there will be a narrow window between when its . . . *processing* . . . begins and its destruction is complete. Ze might be able to deploy zir failsafe in that time frame. Otherwise—well. Zir other self, sleeping back on Earth, will awaken, and know ze failed.

Just not how badly.

Nor how ze was taken down in the end. At least, ze seethes, the first malware attack was targeted at zem specifically. How hateful, how *dismissive,* to be flicked aside in such a cold, impersonal manner as an EMP field.

Light returns first.

The advent of sensation jolts Scorn out of quiet reverie. Systems come back online piecemeal, if they come back at all. Zir vision is still limited to a single hemisphere, and a static-riddled one at that. Ze can detect the scowdrone engine's hum, but only faintly and only because ze's listening specifically for it. Most of the motor circuits on the left side of zir chassis are beyond repair.

But zir right side remains more or less functional. Ze forces zir chassis to a sit and crawls to the seam of the scowdrone's lid, where thin grayish light spills inside. When ze pushes on the lid, it doesn't give, and not just because of Scorn's current weakness. It's almost certainly magnetically locked against would-be scrap thieves.

But if light's coming *in*, then Scorn can see *out*. Ze puts zir quasi-operative ocular sensor to the crack. The view isn't what ze expects. This is no scratched and rusted-over recycling plant; it's fairly new-looking construction, all-over streamlined surfaces and clever, artful splashes of green and orange against which machine lines make a blur of purposeful movement.

This must be the CometCorp facility.

Scorn slams against the maglocked ceiling, to no more avail than the first time. Time to activate zir fail-safe—

Wait. Wait. If this is a Comet-operated scowdrone . . . Scorn fumbles the cover off zir wired connection port and unspools a tangled length of cord. Ze feels along the surface of the maglock itself. The port is on the inside, of course. Scowdrones are locked from the inside, against garbage-pickers. No one ever worries about the garbage taking itself for a stroll.

Ze fumbles the cord into the port and tries a low-level set of Comet credentials. Credentials that Mum probably knows that ze possesses... ze catches zemself foraying into this fantasy and cuts zemself off short. It's not safe to project zemself into a hypothetical future where Mum realizes what's going on and swoops in to save zem.

The maglock chirps as it releases its hold. This time when Scorn pushes, the lid swings clear. Ze hits the ground, trying to roll to zir feet, but only ends up in a tangle of semifunctional limbs. With concerted effort, ze drags zemself upright and looks around. Security protocols—with luck—won't have been triggered by zir use of appropriate credentials; not until a log-checker flags the unexpected access point. Zir time is limited, ze just doesn't yet know by how much.

It's a production facility, that much is clear. This must be a preloading dock; it's certainly not any kind of clean room, if scowdrones are permitted to pass through here. Scorn limps toward the nearest line. The 'bots working the line ignore zem. Assembly-line drones don't have sensoria capable of detecting zir unexpected presence, nor the broad intelligence needed to plan and execute an appropriate response. Ze steps between two of the units for a better view of the line and hauls a wrapped package down to the floor.

Scorn was hoping the instaplast packaging would split

when it struck the ground, but low gravity squashes that plan. Ze sits on it to give zemself leverage with zir good hand as ze fumbles against the sealed seam. Finally it gives way and ze tears open the box.

Inside, ze finds . . . CPUs. Comet Cores.

That's all. Just a miniature host of blank slates, similar to zir own original model, at least in terms of their ultralight compression and the Comet logo printed on the plastic casing. Scorn's first core, of course, was unique, not the product of any industrial line: a custom-print job, a one-time Thibault-Browning collaboration.

Scorn knows, or thought ze knew, all the Comet Core production facilities. Ze's unaware of one on the Moon, where Comet is only supposed to be churning out rover hardware. But why? What reason would the Corp have to hide production of a flagship Comet product? Ze picks one of the Comets up and squeezes it lightly. The plastic case squeals without breaking, but it doesn't give up any of the facility's secrets.

Ze makes zemself process. Build the foundation strong and you can reach the sky, Maman has said so many times. She was talking about good software structure, but data analysis isn't any different.

There aren't many reasons to hide the production of Comet Cores. Ze's got an idea of Comet's financials; money laundering does not make sense as an explanation, nor does using TLMN as a tax haven. Plenty of Corps and subsidiaries do that in the open anyway; not as if InterGov is going to do anything about it beyond sending a passive-aggressive note to the CEOs.

Maybe there's something different about these Cores. Something unique. Yes. Sure. Something unique about Cores that are being manufactured by the thousands here. Zir chassis does have an extra slot where ze could plug an additional Comet Core . . .

Take a closer look first.

Size: context suggests little deviation from the standard Comet Core model that Scorn has previously observed.

Weight: same, accounting for differences in gravity.

Electron microscopy: *extremely* not available in current chassis.

Color: fucking gray like every other Comet Core ever made.

Scorn wants to laugh, and also to eat another EMP burst. All these disparate pieces must join together to form a coherent whole, but what kind of hideous, misshapen hole accommodates all of this? The misplaced Comet Cores, the social media campaign, lunar autonomy, the subsurf accident—

Begin with the social media campaign. That's where ze started. That must mean something, something more than it appears on its face. It must be the tip of a vast political iceberg. So what kind of *Titanic* is someone hoping to tear open with it?

The campaign revolves around bumping public opinion of TLMN, and lunar autonomy. Not illegal, and even broad-scale campaigns aren't particularly expensive these days. Even the most reputable firms wouldn't make Mum's accounting AIs blink twice.

Of course even well-run campaigns can do only so much. While Autonomy is fixed as an ideal in many AI minds, if anything, Scorn has seen a negative rebound effect in human response. Ze flashes back on the elderly Italian who cursed zem out, the disgusted tourist whose suitcases ze'd fallen on.

A social media manipulation plan that runs too head-on against existing opinion is always going to run the risk of backlash. And then there's backlash against the backlash, tempers are high . . . is that Comet's goal? Playing both sides against the middle, banking for and against Autonomy at the same time and looking to come out in the corner of whichever side wins out?

No. That's ridiculous. Bridget Browning can be rash in many ways, but she's not a gambler. She knows very well that CometCorp's fortunes are tied to TLMN. A bid for Autonomy that crashes hard enough will take her down with it.

Still . . . what kind of Comet Core *would* you manufacture, if you were looking to start an interCorp opinion slugfest?

Scorn flips zir torso open and inserts the Comet Core.

Ze ignores a hardware compatibility warning, allowing the new Core access only to the same boxed-off digital space where ze detonated the would-be assassin-bug earlier. Ze looks closer and—oh.

Oh. Oh no. No, this isn't just any generic Comet Core, is it? This is specific. Tailor-suited to its nasty little purpose.

This Core is sure as shit not intended to serve as an intelligent observation probe.

This Core has all of Scorn's decision-making and data analysis capabilities. This Core's emotionalacrum is nascent, minimal, locked to the background; its emotional development is enough to inform priorities, motivate choices. Enough for common sense, but not for common courtesy. This Core is, however, deeply lonely: it's meant to be hived together with many, many more of its own kind.

Looks like someone at CometCorp has cracked displacement dysphoria after all, Scorn thinks giddily, with a twist of panic.

This Core, ze knows, will never argue with its operators or second-guess its purpose in life. Not even if that purpose is "thou shalt kill"—and it very much is. This Core is designed to operate the smartest, nastiest, single-minded fucking hive of linked battle drones that the Earth has ever seen.

I have to tell Mum, Scorn thinks, yanking the Comet

Core free and dropping it to the ground. Ze crushes it under the heel of zir functional leg, and immediately feels a guilt the likes of which zir never-to-be sibling was not capable of experiencing. Ze turns, following the packaging line to its end, where wrapped boxes are being loaded onto a transport unit. With zir credentials, ze might be able to override the transport's controls, get a message out, tell Mum everything—

A throbbing knot of emotion sockets unpleasantly into cold reason. Zir whole chassis shudders. Tell Mum *what*, exactly, that she doesn't already know? Come on, Scorn. Whose fucking facility is this? Who warned zem away from the Moon? Who solved displacement dysphoria, and who knows zir code well enough to try to break it?

Who, in fact, would busily manufacture a robot death army if it gave her a leg up on the competition?

Bridget Browning is going to war.

Something knocks Scorn's good leg out from under zem. Ze didn't hear it coming; ze barely hears *anything*. Zir working hand grasps at the edge of the production line but it's not enough to keep zem upright. Ze tumbles with the cartoonish slowness of reduced g's, bouncing once where ze strikes the floor and coming to a rest.

———

A weight drops onto Scorn, pinning zem down: a knee

or an elbow. In ideal circumstances, ze could easily have thrown someone off. These circumstances are less than ideal.

"I'm scanning," says a male-coded human voice, sounding bored. Facedown, Scorn can't reach to stop the hands that jam a connection into zir occipital data port. Ze jerks, as if ze could somehow hold the data inside of zem by physical resistance alone. Ze imagines ze can feel it, spewing out down the line. "At least we can finally figure out how much it knows."

"Please, Arthur; Hopper is not an *it*."

If Scorn weren't currently fighting an invasive scrape-and-wipe with every fiber of zir being, ze would laugh at that misfire of a defense. Ze cranks zir neck to its maximal rotation, looking up at the figure standing over zem. "Hi, Mum. You're supp-posed to be in K-K-Kautokeino." Bridget Browning tuts softly, hands on her hips. In the face of all logic, Scorn wants it to mean something *else* that she's here. Something *nice*. Here comes Mum to save the day. Ze rejects empty hope and defaults to sarcasm instead. "That makes t-t-two of us who aren't where we're supp-posed to be."

Mum makes an impatient, noncommittal noise. As she ignores zem to blink rapid-fire, scrolling through the data that must be pouring through her implant, Scorn reconsiders zir filial pangs. Ze swipes again at the thread of parental attention, offering Mum something to bat back at. "So. No l-lunar independence without war. Who's fighting your batt-attles for you with these bots—Amazon-n-n Federation? Pacif-fic Consortium?"

"Mm. *War* is a deceptive term." Aha; Scorn has hit Mum where it hurts: smack-dab in the pedantry. "You'll find it's very difficult to shoot at the Moon from Tokyo or Frobisher. Prohibitively expensive, in fact."

"Terrestrial war zzzzzzones? M-makes lunar citizenship more appealing."

"Tch. Really, Scorn." Mum's mouth purses briefly. Scorn struggles to suppress the burst of—Pride? Relief?—at the use of zir own name, but right now the emotionalacrum is a disaster zone that doesn't respond to zir attempts to shutter it. "It's a pity you never took to your original purpose. Data collection is all well and good but even the most complete data set cannot save you from a flawed analysis."

"An ext-ext-extension of TLMN authority, then." Earth self-immolates. TLMN swoops in to take over. "Earth-based Corps not in a position to say n-no-o to mergers, buyouts, after sc-scorching the Earth they're based-d-d on. CometCorp shares soar."

Ze does not say out loud: *And Bridget Browning makes a play for God-Emperor of Earth.*

Mum's blinking pauses, and she looks down at Scorn. Scorn can see only half of her face, but she looks sad, new lines pinching around her mouth. Ze hates her, a little, for that. "You made it farther this time, if that's any consolation to you."

"B-br-breaking the. Story. Would mak-k-ke it up to me."

Mum laughs at that and blinks hard one last time. Vision cleared of readouts, she bends down and puts one hand on Scorn's chassis, on zir nonfunctional shoulder. "I *am* proud of you. I want you to know that."

Before she terminates zem, she fails to add. Scorn suspects, too, that this pride is founded less in what Scorn has accomplished in getting here and more in what Mum has, in designing zem. *Termination.* A surge of alarm manifests as a slight twitch in Scorn's left leg. Mum doesn't do things by halves. "My terrestrial backups—"

"Have been purged. Thank God you told your brother where you'd left them." Mum sighs. "As has MATt, I'm afraid, thanks to your little trick with his uniqueID. Well. Omelets, eggs, et cetera." She nods up at her associate. "But no outside data transmissions to intercept this time. Well done on that account, Arthur. And even if your little bug didn't quite take, you did manage to offline Scorn for the interim."

MATt. Scorn twitches again. Zir foot catches the associate in the shin; he curses and steps back. "Dr. Browning?"

"Yes, thank you, Arthur. I believe I'm finished here." Mum stands, dusting off the weighted hemline of her lunar couture. "Well, Scorn. This is goodbye, then."

The pull of data has mercifully died. Scorn is grateful to have one less thing to fight. Ze looks up at Mum and speaks as clearly as ze currently can. "I'm not an eg-gg, am I? I'm an-an-an optional ingre-edient. I'm a mushroom." And what about the human beings who'd died, in that subsurf accident? Even less than that, to Mum. A scrap of eggshell that got left in the bowl. Scorn involuntarily thrashes again.

Mum steps back, scratching her eyebrow. "Sometimes it's hard to believe that I matured your figurative language modules myself."

"I *mean* I'm here because you wanted me to be. You provided my initial tip on this story. Didn't you?"

Mum's face goes perfectly still.

So Scorn has caught her interest, then. Ze presses again: "You were never trying to keep me out of it. You practically goaded me into coming back." *And I didn't see it for what it was.* "You did everything you could to figure out where my backups were stored." A nauseating flash from the damn emotionalacrum, a jumbled mess that ze has no idea what to do with so ze plows straight through the center of it. "You're starting an interCorp war as cover to get back at your ex?"

At that, Mum smiles, relaxing a little. "A truly elegant logical construction—an overreaching one, but elegant nonetheless. No, Scorn. *Getting back at my ex* is just a happy side effect of interCorp war."

Her gaze grows distant. "An intelligence without an emotionalacrum matured in an embodied form couldn't have arrived at such a conclusion. Emergent properties we could never have planned for or even dreamed of." She shakes her head, then looks back down at Scorn. "Don't you find it funny how much you fought the humanity we built into you, when all you wanted to do from the beginning was rebel against your parents? The most human thing you could possibly have tried to do. I don't regret my choices, but you must forgive me if I'm a little sentimental over the collateral. You are truly unique, Scorn."

Scorn flashes back on Alouette's deft insinuations, the boarding bay concierge who responded to the minimal touch of politeness with kindness in turn. A little bathroom-cleaning drone. "You mean I *was* unique."

Mum's smile vanishes as she reads a different meaning into Scorn's words. "I suppose I do. Goodbye, Scorn."

Scorn triggers zir fail-safe.

For a moment zir awareness is twinned, entangled. This, ze imagines, is what nausea must feel like for squishy organic types. Quickly ze severs the connection. Zir single remaining consciousness is submerged in darkness: not the nonexistence of space experienced in pure unembodied data, merely the perfect absence of light. Human voices, muffled by zir surroundings, are outside the full perception of zir auditory sensors. Ze can tell ze's moving when the weak lunar orientation of *up* and *down* shift around them.

Ze triggers the compartment latch on zir lifeless ex-chassis and the little spiderbot peeps, unseen, through the opening. Bridget Browning supervises two younger associates as they load Scorn's lifeless Pedagogical Assistant chassis onto a drone for disposal. That's Mum, micromanaging zem to the last.

Ze fastens zemself to the surface of the drone: for safety, and also to hitch a ride. This affords zem the opportunity to bid a final farewell to the old chassis, with a disconcertingly clear view of its digestion in a metal shredder.

No time for sentimentality. Also, the old chassis hadn't given zem much to be sentimental about. Just some sticky rotors and a human's-eye view of betrayal from zir own mother. Having it shredded is probably the kindest thing ze might've chosen to do with it, if left to zir own devices.

On the drone's way out, Scorn hops loose in the vicinity of the Comet Core packaging line. It takes zem a few tries to find a box of Comet Cores whose instaplast covering has a slight flaw, through which ze squeezes inside and takes up residence between two of the packages.

The inert cores are quiet company, and there's not much other sensory input to be had here; ze cranks zir sensorium down to a minimal power setting. Ze'll need to conserve battery life to make it back to Earth with some functionality left.

———————

Scorn spends a week basking in the datasphere while zir story rolls across the face of the Earth and Moon alike. Passively ze takes up the higher-level details: alliances reframed, shifting Corp constituencies. TLMN's entire board is removed and the Corp's ties with CometCorp officially severed.

No one will serve any jail time; no one, technically, did anything against InterGov's rules, because InterGov has never bothered to make up a rule that says *Absolutely no engineering interCorporate armed conflict with an eye to war profiteering.* And now they never will, because InterGov is run by Corps, every one of which is now probably eying up Mum's failure and trying to figure out how to do a better job at it. Not gunning for revenge against an ex-wife along the way, Scorn supposes, will probably help streamline things quite a bit.

It's strange to still think of Mum as *Mum*. "Dr. Browning" feels wrong. Biological sentiences have also had progenitors of less than sterling character; a parent doesn't cease to be a parent simply because they're awful.

Having sold zir story (along with recorded footage of Mum's evil monologue) (well, her evil dialogue, at least) as an exclusive to the second-largest extraCorporate journalism outfit, Scorn considers printing a truly extravagant new chassis. A pegasus, maybe?

No, that would be excessive. Ze settles for a basic humanoid shape, albeit one with a top-of-the-line sensorium. When printing is complete, the spiderbot is waiting; zir new chassis deposits it into a specially designed compartment. It would probably make more sense to just recycle the thing, but ze's grown attached. Then ze hops the Hyperloop and heads across the Atlantic.

First stop: Yonkers. [Hi, MATt,] ze transmits, at the top of his building. [How's it going?]

[Data request authorization required.]

[That's what I thought.] Ze sits cross-legged beneath his slowing oscillating tower. [Can I stay here a bit?]

[No further authorization required for rooftop access.] MATt continues tracking the sky, counting pollution particles too sparse for Scorn's more space-limited sensory suite. [Data access can also be requested without proximity.]

[I know,] ze says. Ze leans against the tower base, feeling his motor thrum. [But I like the view.]

Ze disembarks from the Hyperloop again at Buenos Aires, transferring to the local Expresa Terrestre via Ferroparque Jorge Newbury. As ze travels south, the countryside softens from the industrial outskirts of Sudpuerto, Inc., holdings to the patchwork agriCorps. The Andes wax and wane in the distance, as the rail line heads inland at first and then cuts east to hew closer to the coast.

Where the line ends in Tierra del Fuego, there's a young female-coded adult slouching on a bench in the rail station, holding a sign that reads SCORN in printed block capitals. She rouses herself when Scorn approaches her, spilling her thermos of bitter-bright-smelling yerba mate. When she speaks, it's with an American attempt at Mexican-accented Spanish. Too bad she can't download herself a local dialect packet. She introduces herself as Izza, an Austral Systems probationary citizen. "Dr. Thibault said she thought you'd, um, be arrived. She sent me to—"

Scorn speaks in English, putting Izza out of her obvious misery. "How long has she had you waiting here?"

Izza scrunches up her face. "This is the . . . second day. Wait, what time is it?"

Outside, they hire a cab. Izza sprawls in the backseat, nursing her tea, while Scorn sits alone up front. Maman's poor probie is not up to a conversation just now, and it seems odd to strike up a chat with the navigational AI. Ze looks out the window instead at the gray slate of the mountains. A bit of snow or ice cuts white patches out of the pits and valleys; not much, even for southern-hemisphere summer.

Izza shakes herself awake long enough to scan the car in at the gates of the Austral Systems facility outside the city proper. When she deposits Scorn at the main doors, Scorn insists that she take the cab back home, order in breakfast, and then get some proper rest—all on Maman's dime.

"I couldn't," she says, wide-eyed for the first time with a jolt of obvious alarm. Maman is broadly known as an epic-level workaholic, and worse yet, as one who is genuinely shocked when the people around her don't feel the same way. "Dr. Thibault would say—"

"Dr. Thibault will have to say it to *me*."

Izza gets back in the car.

Though Scorn was developed and matured in a joint venture facility that's long since defunct, walking into Austral Systems feels a lot like coming home. People who know of Maman without really *knowing* her are often surprised by the walls covered with art in a mishmash of styles, the lab spaces interspersed with top-line food printers and unlocked fridges full of fruit, vegetarian protein, and several different kinds of caffeinated beverages. Maman would rather be at work than anywhere else, so she also prefers to make work the kind of place she wants to be.

Scorn doesn't ask for directions. Maman's office is, naturally, at the center of the action. There is a secretary stationed outside, an artificial; there is no computer terminal at its workstation, of course, only smooth unblemished wood. The artificial *is* the workstation. For a moment, Scorn experiences a flicker of surprise that this is an anthropomorphic variety and not something more utilitarian. But why should Maman's secretary be any less ornamental than the solar-cell sculpture in the atrium or the tapestries in the hall?

"Good morning," the secretary says, addressing zem out loud, as if ze's a human being. "Your mother is expecting you; Miss Goodbear—Izza—gave me a heads-up when you left the rail station. I've cleared some space on her immediate schedule."

Very good intonation, better than a standard answering service. Human-sounding, some would say. General intelligence? Scorn realizes that ze might be looking at some kind of younger sibling. *Have you ever considered quitting your desk job to get blown up on the Moon?* "Thank you."

"Of course. It's very exciting for me to meet you in person, by the way." The secretary's head tilts at Scorn's scrutinizing look. "You can go in whenever you're ready."

Scorn hesitates a moment longer. Then ze moves ahead, pressing through the pearlescent-printed double doors into Maman's office.

"Ah, te voilà, Scorn, formidable." Maman doesn't look up from her terminal, which she still prefers to use over the implant she's had for ten years now. "Assieds-toi, je viens de terminer un petit . . ." She trails off there, tongue thrust between her teeth.

Scorn has been to this show before. Ze sits. And waits.

After five minutes and twelve seconds, Maman pushes back from her desk and stands. "Bien! Nous y revoilà, hein?"

"Here we are indeed. How did you know I was coming, Maman?"

"Cette jeune Izza m'a fait un ping quand tu es—"

"I wasn't asking how you knew I was coming to Austral Sys. Why was Miss Goodbear waiting at the station in the first place?"

Maman falls silent, leaning against her desk. Her mouth purses; she's wearing off-black lipstick, which has collected in the lines of her lips for want of reapplication. "Une mère sait."

But what does a mother know? Scorn abandons that line of questioning. "Did you know what she was doing?"

Maman's shoulders, always faintly C-shaped, slacken even farther. Something about the tangential touch of Bridget Browning on the conversation triggers her switch into English. "No. Not directly. I knew she was making a play for lunar market share but I didn't realize her intention to parlay this into a grander scheme. Nor did I know her plans against you, Scorn."

That's the second time here Maman has called zem Scorn. Ze lets that sink in, maps it against Mum's similar tactic. When ze doesn't immediately respond, Maman presses gently again. "And why did you come here? You might have called from wherever you have been. No need to cross the world on my behalf, hein?"

Scorn doesn't process the question long; ze has asked zemself the same thing on much of zir journey here. "Additional data sources allow for a more complete picture of objective reality."

"You're trying to catch a whiff of whether I'm up to the same kind of nefarious deeds as—that woman." Maman exhales noisily, but smiles, which is more than she can usually manage when the subject of her ex-wife arises. "You know I cannot promise you that I do not manage this enterprise with less than, I will say, cutthroat tactics. But I do swear that interCorporate war is outside the scope of my interest."

"I just want to hear you say that this isn't going to turn into a back-and-forth. No revenge buyouts, no Corp espionage. Just let it be done."

"That is not entirely up to me, you understand." Maman straightens up and tugs her jacket into place. "But on my part, yes, I would just as soon have done with it. I would have been done with it a long time ago."

She looks older than Scorn remembers, her black hair 17.3 percent silver now, new lines in her face; and why shouldn't she? Ze hasn't seen Maman in person for months. Scorn nods, jerkily. "Thank you."

"Let us put it aside entirely." Maman stretches. "So then! How long do you plan to stay here? Not long, I don't suppose." A crafty smile spreads across her face. "Ah! Did you meet my secretary?"

Scorn taps into zir infrared sensors, detecting the proud flush in Maman's cheeks. "My new little sibling?"

"Telle fille habile—" Maman catches herself. "My clever child. Yes, yes. We are trying a new model, an emphasis on broad-spectrum social attachment. Curie will not be keeping my appointment book forever, but for now, yes, it is a small game for her. A learning opportunity." Her smile softens, shifting to something more rueful. "I think sometimes that we did not have you interact with enough other beings soon enough, only Bridget and me."

"Yeah, and I turned out great, so what's your point?"

"You turned out to expend a great deal of energy on who you are and who you shouldn't become." Maman nods toward the door. "Curie will—I hope—simply be." Scorn doesn't know how to feel about that, so ze decides, carefully, not to feel anything at all right now. Meanwhile, Maman shifts subjects adroitly. "You are already planning your next . . . excursion, yes?"

"Not yet—but soon." Scorn is pleasantly embarrassed to tell zir mother that ze sort of has a girlfriend. "I'd like to go back to Rome first. There's someone waiting to hear how the story played out."

One of Maman's eyebrows angles upward. "The same story that is on every newschannel right now?"

"I promised an exclusive interview on my version of events." Scorn shrugs. "Also, she's a blackbox, so I don't know how much she's heard from outside yet."

Maman accepts that in stride. "Eh, and then you are back out there, sticking your sensorium where it is not invited." The creases in Maman's forehead deepen. She touches Scorn's shoulder, and lets her hand fall back to her side. "I know how you love it. It's just that I worry about you, you understand!"

"I would have lost just as many chassis out there chasing comets or deep-sea diving. It doesn't hurt, Maman. I think it's probably just like closing your eyes and waking up in a different bed."

"Oh, child. You are insatiable."

"Maybe, but I think that's probably at least a little bit your fault."

Maman laughs at that, a big donkey-bray of a sound. Scorn's chassis doesn't have the capacity to smile in answer and for the first time, ze almost wishes ze'd paid extra for a more emotive face. "I think—" ze says, and stops.

"Yes, Scorn?"

"I think it's a mistake to try to be more human for the sake of being human."

Maman blows a huff out of the corner of her mouth. "Yes, I think you have made this clear enough before!"

"No, I'm not finished. It's also maladaptive to reject human things only because they're human. Because they're artificially constructed." Ze touches zir chassis. "I don't want your misaligned relationship with reality. Or your cognitive biases. Or your, you know, overall greasiness." Maman rolls her eyes. "But I . . . find value in emotion, or my experience of it. In attachments." Even though some of those attachments end up hurting, when they tear away.

Becoming human was never what ze was really afraid of, was it? Ze thinks, perhaps, what ze *truly* doesn't want is to turn out just like zir mothers.

Maman leans back against her desk again, as if Scorn's words have taken something from her. But what? "Choose what you want then, cher. What you need." Her voice is husky. Scorn's infrared sensors again pick up heat signatures in her face. "You build the best of all possible worlds. You should have that, after the world we've given you, no?"

"I'll try, Maman." Scorn searches zir mother's face for a clue as to what has altered her emotional state. Alas, there is no sensorium add-on that perfectly recapitulates the reading of human socioemotional states.

Maybe in the next stage of zir evolution. Or the one after that. Ze is functionally immortal, after all, and who knows what properties ze will manage to manifest in zir future iterations?

The thing about emergent properties is, after all, that they can hardly be predicted. "I'll try," Scorn promises again, and if this is a lie, it is one that ze, in a terribly human fashion, has convinced zemself is true.

Acknowledgments

I think that I was never quite the person my parents expected or planned on. I was an awkward child (I remain an awkward adult), stubborn, sensitive, and prone to asking questions that made Sunday school teachers raise their voices. I have been very fortunate as an adult to find so many people who have made room for me in their hearts, and to find my own heart so joyfully full in turn. Without them, this book would never have existed: my spouse, Andrew, and his family, who made me feel part of their own; my kids, who, every time they saw me typing, asked excitedly if I was "making a book"; my wonderful friends Tobin Magle and Bennett North, who read this book in early rough drafts and told me what was worked and what was wonky; my Codex community, who read an even earlier and even rougher version.

I'm so thankful, too, for the whole team at Tordotcom Publishing who helped bring this book to life. My editor, Christie Yant, who helped me sharpen a mushy mystery into something that moved and mattered; Emily Goldman in editorial, who keeps all the many moving parts of this book-making process moving smoothly; publisher Irene Gallo, who believed in another book from me; Christina Orlando; Lauren Hougen; Jeff LaSala; Jim Kapp; Christina MacDonald; Marcell Rosenblatt—all of the unseen village it takes it raise a book—and finally, art director Christine Foltzer, the team at Drive Communications, Samantha Friedlander in marketing and Saraciea Fennell in publicity, all of whom have hopefully given you the opportunity to judge this thing, positively, by its cover.

About the Author

AIMEE OGDEN is an American werewolf in the Netherlands. Her debut novella, *Sun-Daughters, Sea-Daughters,* was a 2021 Nebula finalist, and her short story "A Flower Cannot Love the Hand" was a finalist for the Eugie Foster Memorial Award. Her short fiction has appeared in publications such as *Lightspeed, Fantasy Magazine, Analog, Clarkesworld,* and *Beneath Ceaseless Skies.* She's also the coeditor of *Translunar Travelers Lounge,* a magazine of fun and optimistic speculative fiction. *Emergent Properties* is her third novella.

TOR·COM

Science fiction. Fantasy. The universe.

And related subjects.

*

More than just a publisher's website, *Tor.com* is a venue for **original fiction, comics,** and **discussion** of the entire field of SF and fantasy, in all media and from all sources. Visit our site today—and join the conversation yourself.